THE ICE IDOLS

A novel by

Paul Jones

Copyright 2022

'Sir, we live in a damned wicked world and the fewer we praise, the better.' – School for Scandal, Richard Brinsley Sheridan

'Satan's first words are about how talented we are.' - Clive James

'What profit is an idol?' - Habbakuk 2:18

Also by Paul Jones:

Scratch, The Spy Detector, Actor's Intelligence and Thieves and Ghosts.

Copyright © Paul Jones 2022 All rights reserved.

Published by Paul Jones/ lulu.com

ISBN 978-1-4478-2809-9

The Ice Idols

CHAPTER ONE

You always knew when Leonard Newton had arrived. The first time Troy Colson met him he thought, *Now that's what I call an actor.* It made Troy wonder if Leonard had something that he hadn't. Troy was an actor too and he had a degree to prove it.

The two men had known each other vaguely while studying at the Royal Academy of Dramatic Arts. Troy had joined in 1998, a year after Leonard. And now here they were, three years later, on a dull September day at the Nottingham Ice Arena. They were obviously both auditioning for *Ice Idols*, a prospective Saturday night some-singing, some-dancing but mainly ice-skating extravaganza for the BBC. Not for nothing had they studied the plays of Strindberg and Samuel Beckett. No time had been wasted in learning to analyse character or to develop process and motivation. Here was the big one and they were both ready for it.

In the little piazza near the entrance to the Motorpoint Ice Centre, there was a multicoloured autumnal swirl of yellow and brown leaves, blue and green crisp packets and various shapes and sizes of cigarette cartons. Troy pulled open the stiff entrance door, but before he could go in, Leonard had walked through it as if Troy were the doorman. He turned to look at him.

'Thanks, mate. I know you, don't I? Don't tell me, don't tell me! Ronnie?'
'Troy,' said the other man as he came through the door behind Leonard. Leonard was the only man in the world with a fruity Yorkshire accent. If he felt demeaned by the prospect of becoming a skating celebrity, he didn't show it.

'Troy Colson.'

'That's the one!' Leonard replied, his voice booming and reverberating in the foyer. They both shook hands. Troy winced: Leonard had a grip like Giant Haystacks.

Troy remembered Leonard doing *Richard III* at RADA. He had envied his stage presence and his magnetism with the girls. He seemed to be going places in the world of theatre. And here he was, like Troy, with a pair of skates around his neck. It was at this moment that Troy realised something quite extraordinary: he was a good four or five inches taller than Leonard. It was a tribute to the other man's charisma that he had never noticed it before. He had always thought of Leonard as a giant.

'So, how's tricks, matey? Dragged you up to Nottingham, have they?'

'Actually,' said Troy, 'I'm from around here. I live in London, but I stayed at my mum's last night because...'

'...Can you really skate?'

'Well enough. You?'

'Same. If we end up on our backsides then we can audition for *Casualty*, eh?'

Leonard laughed loudly at his own witticism and Troy saw no reason not to join him. In the foyer was a young BBC assistant who showed them into the gigantic ice stadium. The rink was empty apart from a man and a woman who skated over to the seating and checked their names.

'Newton, Leonard. 9.00am. Colson, Troy, 9.15am. Take a seat if you can find one - ha ha - and we'll call you shortly.'

Both the interviewers glided over the ice with the effortless ease of wraiths in a graveyard, perhaps just to make the actors feel as silly as possible. The only other person in the entire auditorium was a third production assistant, a solemn-looking man who sat at the ringside and was either making notes or writing a suicide letter. Probably the latter, since he expressed no interest in any of the candidates and said not a word to anyone. Leonard and Troy both wondered if the places had already been filled and they were just going through the motions for a final day's expenses.

'Is this it?' asked Troy, waving a hand at all the empty seats.

'We've been interviewing for five days,' said the clipboard man. 'Today was just an extra day for the few that spilled over.'

They both thought that this confirmed their suspicions. Troy nodded and said,

'This is actually the warmest audition room I've ever been in.'

'We're expecting eight today,' said the clipboard girl. 'That probably means four will turn up.' Then she added, 'Get your skates on lads – literally.'

They did as they were told. While they were getting organised, the two actors got an opportunity to size each other up. They were both brown-haired, but whereas Troy's was mouse brown, Leonard's was rich, thick and dark like the coat of a wild Kodiak. He was powerfully built to match. Troy was good-looking, but not in any forceful or charismatic way. He had more like the sort of protein-deficient, telegenic aspect of some popular politicians. Mothers would have thought him handsome when he was young. He was one of those men who would be eternally youthful. If he was not careful, he would end up on children's television. (If he could play the guitar then his doom was assured.) Yes, he could do Shakespeare. He would have made a good Antonio in *The Merchant of Venice,* but probably not a Hamlet and never in an age Macbeth.

Now Leonard could play Macbeth and any other dark part. It wouldn't be so easy to see him playing comedy, although you could imagine him arguing with the director about the function of humour in psycho-sociological terms. And you could imagine the rest of the cast looking at their watches and rolling their eyes when he said he had a few ideas for developing the role of Dick Whittington in the Christmas panto. But he was friendly enough, even if he did monopolise the conversation.

'Been up to much, matey?'

'Did an advert this year,' said Troy, keeping his sentences short in the hope that he would be able to finish them.

'Corn plasters, was it?'

'It *was* corn plasters!' Troy was impressed. 'They gave me the job because...'

'...Thought it was. Did a couple myself this year. Bloody good payers. And I had a *Romeo and Juliet* over in the East End. Went very well but didn't transfer. Bad director. Bad marketing. Usual stuff. I was good, of course.'

'Who was Juliet?'

But there was no reply.

Troy couldn't remember seeing Leonard in any adverts, but then he wasn't a big television watcher. And there were lots of other places you could show an advert these days. Troy didn't figure Leonard for a liar.

Quite the opposite: he was obviously the sort of man who could tell you he'd done a photo-shoot for lice powder as if he had starred in *The Lion King* on Broadway for a year.

'Shirley Gollancz?' said the clipboard lady. '9.30?'

But there was no Shirley Gollancz. Her name was crossed spitefully off the list.

Troy watched as Leonard took his turn, skating competently at first but slipping when he tried to get a bit fancy. After they had checked that he was not hurt, they helped him back to his seat.

''I'll give Casualty a ring,' said Troy, but that was not the sort of joke which Leonard appreciated. Instead, he explained that the ice was not kept at the correct temperature.

'Yeah, I'm sure that's it,' said Troy.

Troy was called next and did pretty much the same performance as Leonard. He didn't actually slip over but may have pulled something as he tried to do a complicated spin manoeuvre. He went and sat down again.

'Two of us for Casualty, eh?' said Leonard, winking – and the joke was funny again.

The clipboard lady looked up at the vast emptiness of the auditorium and said, 'Gloria Greatorex?'

The two actors were very impressed by the way Gloria appeared from nowhere as if she had been waiting for a theatre cue. Troy and Leonard were taking off their skates and talking about taking the train back to London together when Gloria said,

'Don't go boys. I need an audience.'

She spoke in the strangely clipped accent of a 1950s quiz contestant.

It was not easy for healthy young men to refuse Gloria anything. She was groomed to perfection for an audition, with a shiny plastic sheen of make-up – much more than a highly attractive nineteen-year-old really needed - and her long blonde hair tightly tied up behind her in a ponytail. She had an immaculate face, without blemish or wrinkle. Without a doubt she was very beautiful, if your tastes did not run to the natural country girl look. She didn't give the impression of having bathed in a clear mountain cataract; but you could imagine her lying on a slab covered in mineral mud, with energy stones placed strategically across her body and with two slices of creamed mango on the eyes. She was wearing a blue padded jumpsuit, as if she expected trouble on the ice. She noticed Leonard first and spoke directly to him. Troy felt himself disappearing. It was a sensation he had encountered before. If Gloria had had a girlfriend with her, she too would have been invisible.

Leonard and Troy dutifully resumed their seats. Gloria donned her skates and glided out onto the ice. Like the two men, she could skate competently in a straight line but found more inventive manoeuvring a challenge. She wobbled on the turns but got through the audition without falling. The clipboard couple kept looking at their watches. They wanted to be gone. It was not often that they ventured out of London, and they were perhaps concerned about picking up alien infections. They may have been surprised when, on arriving in the Midlands, they had not been mobbed by groups of street traders selling chickens or home-made dentures.

'Nobody else?' said the distaff clipboard.

There was nobody else.

'Jolly good,' said the clipboard man. 'Thanks children. Let you know through the usual channels.'

And that was that. Troy, Leonard, Gloria and the BBC assistants trooped up the aisle to the exit. That was when Shirley Gollancz appeared. She looked like someone in a hurry. Her mane of basalt black hair was all over the place. She resembled a lovely dark bird of prey, ready to swoop down on some unsuspecting field mouse who had offended her by being too deferential. She probably lived in a beach hut made from the skulls of flatterers. Her long black dress seemed not appropriate to the occasion.

'Shirley Gollancz,' she said firmly, as if that were the only explanation she would ever need for anything.

'The audition's over,' said the clipboard lady, but with not enough conviction to deter someone who could clearly smell fear.

'No, it isn't,' said Shirley. 'You're still here.'

'Yes,' said her clipboard colleague, 'but you were meant to be here at 9.30.'

'I thought it was 10.30,' said Shirley. 'I'm sure it was 10.30. Anyway, I'm here now.'

She pointed at the ice and walked down toward it. Everyone obediently followed. Clearly, she was going to get the audition through sheer force of personality. She pointed to Gloria.

'I'm so glad you're here: I'll need to borrow your skates.'

Gloria was stunned.

'Don't you have any of your own?'

'No. Never really needed any. I think they're a waste of money.'
'You *can* skate, can't you?' asked the clipboard man, looking worried and thinking perhaps of lawsuits. Shirley looked at him for a moment and then decided he was an irrelevance. She concentrated on putting on Gloria's skates. Then she added to herself,
'It doesn't look that difficult.'
Everyone else exchanged glances. It was clear that Shirley had never skated before. That was even clearer when she went out onto the ice. It was a bit more difficult than she had imagined. She fell over a couple of times but got up again and persevered. The clipboard people said nothing. (Whether this was through fear or a desire for revenge as Shirley hurt herself, was a moot point.) Eventually she wobbled back to the rink side.
'There. That was easy. Shouldn't be too difficult to pick that up.'
'Oh, definitely not,' said the clipboard lady. 'You'll be ready in at least a month, I should say. Can we go now?'
'I'm not stopping you,' said Shirley.
Leonard must have thought that Shirley had been the centre of attention now for too long.
'Right,' he said picking up his bag, 'who's for the station?'
'I've got an empty car,' said Shirley to Gloria, Leonard and Troy, 'if you're all going to London.'
'You can *drive*, can't you?' asked Gloria.
'Yes, I can drive.'

They were all going to London. They packed up and followed Shirley. The two skating interviewers left. But the man sitting writing at the ringside remained. Nobody seemed to know who he was.

None of them ever heard about the audition. *Ice Idols* was never made. They made a quiz show about horse racing instead. That wasn't much good either.

CHAPTER TWO

The best description of Shirley's car would be that it was cosy. Usually advertised on television as a 'runabout' or 'nippy in traffic', it was hardly the optimal conveyance for transporting four actors and their various impedimenta – not to mention four personalities which would have felt cramped in a jumbo jet. The tight conditions meant that their loud voices seemed to be squeezed up against everyone else's. Eventually, they had to shout to be heard.

'I auditioned once for an ad for *Persil*.'

'Oh, I did that too! Or was it *Daz*?'

'Didn't you get it?'

'*I* would have got it.'

'Then why didn't you go for it?'

'I was busy.'

'Or was it *Aerial*? One of those.'

'No wonder you didn't get it if you couldn't remember the name.'

'You always think any product is the market leader. I read that.'

'My agent messed it up.'

'*Your* agent? You should have my agent.'

'It was *Persil*. I remember now.'

'One advert can set you up for life.'

'You mean get you into a type-casting rut for ever.'

'You can say that about any role.'

'You can't say it about anything. If the money is good in an ad, it allows you to go for better roles. You can relax and not take rubbish.'

'What do you mean rubbish? Most ads are rubbish.'

'Most ads are brilliant. They're better than the shows.'

It was the conversational equivalent of a pinball machine. Eventually Troy called for quiet.

'Hold it, everyone! Let's get to know each other. There's a better way to do it. Everybody tell one story.'

'What story?'

'Any story. A story about you. Don't go on, just a few minutes. Anything. Shirley – you start.'

'Me? I'm driving. I can't think. I'll go after everyone else.'

'Gloria.'

'Any story?'

'Sure.'

'Keep it clean,' said Leonard. 'Troy is very innocent.'

'Well, when I was working in New York...'

'There!' said Troy. 'We didn't know you'd lived in America.'

'No interruptions.'

'When I was working in New York last year, I was a temp at this show biz agency. Big agency it was. And one day I answered the phone saying 'Gloria' and this guy on the other end of the phone thought I was Gloria Gaynor. He spoke to me for a few minutes thinking I was Gloria Gaynor. He was like really embarrassed when I told him.'

There was a pause after this tale. Troy filled in by saying 'interesting'. Like the other two in the car, he suspected that this story might not be quite true since Gloria Gaynor would have had a very different accent from Gloria Greatorex. But they said nothing.

'Leonard.'

Leonard's story was routine. In fact, the content could have been guessed at. It was one of those 'darling, I said' stories. The gist of it was that Leonard had met some great actor who had said something demeaning to Leonard and he had retaliated with some whiplash rejoinder which had put the man in his place. It was probably partly true. Leonard probably really had met the man in question, but he may have only thought of his reply a couple of hours later.

'You next, Troy,' said Shirley.

'My story is this. When I was a teenager – about twelve or thirteen – I was alone in the house one evening. My father had already deserted us and my mother was out working. I switched on the telly. There was a film on. It had already started so I missed the opening credits. I didn't know until later it was called *Blow Up,* and I'd never heard of it or the star, David Hemmings. The first thing I saw was a large group of workmen coming out of a factory at home time. They were all dressed in boiler suits. But I saw David Hemmings and I noticed him. He stood out. I'd never seen him before, but I picked him out. I knew he was the main character. That was when I knew why stars got paid so much. They really have to have that quality.'

Troy told this tale with a poignant and regretful tone.

'I don't get it,' said Shirley. 'Are you saying that's why you became an actor?'

'Are you saying that's why you *shouldn't* be an actor?' asked Leonard.

'Not necessarily. It was just a story. And it's true.'

'That should have been my story,' said Leonard.

'And mine,' said Gloria.

'But it happened to Troy,' said Shirley. Then she said, 'Me now. I've got one.'

Shirley's story was that when she was a teenager, she and her girlfriends had selected numbers from the phone book and called them. If a young woman answered, they would say, *I've been sleeping with your husband.*

She told this short tale as if it were humorous and endearing.

'Oh, Shirley, you didn't!' said Gloria. But that was the fullest extent of anyone's outrage.

'That wasn't about acting,' said Leonard.

'Nobody said it had to be. Just stories, we said.'

'No,' said Leonard decisively. 'It has to be about showbusiness or acting.'

'No, it did not! You're inventing rules...what's that word where you go backwards?'

'Retrospectively,' said Troy.

'Yes, that's it. You're making rules retrospectively.'

'All right,' said Troy helpfully. 'What's your philosophy, Shirley?'

'Oh, that's easy. I follow what Clint Eastwood said: go for any job. If they ask if you can ride a motorcycle over a cliff, say *Yes, I can ride a motorbike over a cliff.* Just go for it.'

'You mean *carpe diem*,' said Troy. 'Seize the day. Seize any opportunity?'

'Yes, I think so.'

'That's a dangerous outlook,' said Gloria.

'I don't care,' said Shirley.

Everyone believed her. Honour was satisfied.

But Shirley continued, 'Danger only happens to other people. You have to grab every opportunity without thinking. The world stays the same. Opportunity is always present.'

'What if there's a war?'

'Then you go somewhere else. Look at World War Two. Sweden and Switzerland went on as normal. So did Portugal – I think.'

'What if there's World War Three?'

'There won't be; not while I'm alive,' she said. This was quite a claim.

After that, the conversation became a bit more sedate, a bit less competitive. Nobody had to jostle to establish himself anymore. It was the afternoon when they got back to Shirley's flat in Walthamstow and she invited them in for coffee.

The flat was impressive. It was one of those ridiculously opulent pads that people on television live in but you never see in real life – unless you mixed with hedge fund owners. It was the only flat they had ever seen where you didn't wonder how they got the furniture in. It testified to independent means.

The lounge and dining room were combined, but you could have easily played a game of badminton doubles in it. The decoration was mostly restrained. On the far wall was a Fabian Perez painting of a *film noir* setting. It showed dark men and women from the forties, and was quite out of place in the bright, white room. A simple abstract by Mondrian would have been more suited to the décor. Or better still, a map of the London Underground. But the picture was probably an original.

Shirley made coffee in the spotless kitchenette while Troy and Gloria tested an assortment of luxurious white seats.

'This is different from what I expected,' said Leonard, pacing about like a pirate king on deck. He may have felt threatened by the expanse of the place.

'What did you expect?' asked Shirley through the serving hatch.

'I don't know. I think I expected to see skiing equipment or painting materials all over the shop.'

'I have the use of the shed for that. What's your flat like?'

Leonard shrugged evasively. Troy said,

'My flat's like your shed. Except your shed is probably bigger. And probably tidier too. And I don't have any painting equipment.'

'I paint,' said Gloria.

'Oh, right,' said Troy, 'what do you paint?'

'Apart from your toenails,' said Shirley. Gloria tried to raise her eyebrows at this, but they were not designed for mobility.

'This and that,' she answered. She tried to tell them but became vague and drifted into general comments about art. The others assumed that she didn't really paint at all.

'Come and look at my etchings sometime,' said Leonard as he plumped down on the rich, soft sofa next to her.

'I will,' she said, looking directly at him.

Gloria untied her blonde hair and shook it loose. There was plenty of it. It was only then that Leonard recognised her as the girl from the *Discount Furniture Warehouse* commercial. She was flattered that he recognised her. They started to chat quietly to each other, and they both turned out to live in the same area, she in Streatham and he in Tooting. They agreed to meet some time.

'Sadly, I don't live near you,' said Troy to Shirley as she came in with the coffee tray and sat opposite him in one of the armchairs. He leaned over towards her to make his point.

'We can still meet,' she said with a forwardness which Troy found disconcerting. (Men are always claiming how much easier it would be if women approached *them*, but when it happens they are always knocked off balance.)

'I live in Sudbury Town,' he said.

'Never heard of it.'

'No, it's not famous for anything. I doubt if they'll be doing the *Antiques Roadshow* there any time soon. We do have a sports centre, although I don't get too close to it. But it is near Wembley.'

'Is that good or bad?'

'Finds autographed footballs in his garden, don't you…er…Troy,' said Leonard.

'Oh, please, call me Ronnie.'

'Switch the telly on,' said Leonard. 'See what the news is.'

Leonard was a man who gave orders and Shirley was a woman who didn't take them. She ignored him.

'I'll come over, if that's OK,' said Troy. They made a date too.

He picked up the TV console and said, 'Do you mind?'

Shirley didn't mind and he switched it on. BBC1 seemed to be showing some kind of disaster movie which none of them recognised. It was an odd time to be showing one. There appeared to be a large skyscraper on fire.

'Try the other one,' said Leonard. Troy pressed for BBC2 and could see the same thing.

'You pressed the wrong button,' said Leonard. Troy pressed some others. They all showed the same thing. All four of them watched in bewilderment.

'That's the World Trade Centre, isn't it?' said Shirley suspiciously.

Gloria, who had apparently lived in New York, said she wasn't sure.

'Erm…folks…' said Troy slowly, 'I think this is really happening.'

They looked at each other. Then Gloria screamed as the second plane hit the second tower. There were a few obscene exclamations, but mainly they were lost for words.

'Oh bloody hell!' Gloria shouted after a while. 'All those people! There must be hundreds in there!'

'Hundreds? Thousands.'

Along with the whole world, they watched for a long time, fascinated and horrified, long after the possibility of learning anything new. Somehow, nobody wanted to leave. This was not a time to be sitting alone in some dingy bedsit. The terrible event seemed to have formed a bond which was stronger than nascent friendships and romantic attractions. Somehow it seemed inappropriate and unfeeling to drink their coffee. It was an hour before they realised they were hungry. They ordered pizzas and waited.

'What's your philosophy now, Shirley?' said Gloria quietly.

'The same: it's terrible, but things go back to normal. Nothing changes.'

'Except for the dead,' said Leonard.

'Not after World War Three,' said Troy.

'There won't be a war, will there?' asked Gloria, even paler than normal. Troy answered himself quickly.

'No, of course not. There's no-one to bomb. These people are phantoms.'

'What people?' said Leonard. 'You don't know who did it.'

'I bet they do. I bet they know exactly who it is. These things are never surprises. I don't know what they'll do now.'

'I don't mean to be callous,' said Shirley, 'but things *do* go back to normal.'

'For the survivors.'

'Not for their relatives.'

'Yes, it does eventually. The food will be here soon and we'll eat and life will go on. It won't abolish the future.'

They started to talk about the future, seriously at first - but the erratic drift of their conversation confirmed Shirley's opinion. They started with the philosophy of time and what it meant. Then they ended up talking about their favourite science fiction movies. They began discussing them quietly and guiltily at first, but soon became animated. It passed the time. The pizzas arrived and provided another avenue of conversation. They switched off the television and the first stage of removal was complete.

Eventually, Gloria said, 'This is a real moment. We should never forget this. I mean forget that we met on this occasion.'

'Agreed,' said Leonard. He said 'agreed' as if he were saying 'approved' or 'permission granted'.

Gloria continued, 'We should never lose touch.'

Troy nodded, but he looked a little concerned, as if this horror was becoming a tad too much about *them*. But he agreed out loud and so did Shirley. Then Gloria said,

'We should meet again in five years. Have a meal or something. Regardless...regardless of where we are or what we're doing.'

'Even if we're not friends anymore?' asked Shirley.

'Even if we're mortal enemies,' said Leonard, putting the final seal on it. 'We can keep track of each other and see if Shirley's theory is correct.'

'What theory?'

'That danger only happens to other people.'

'I haven't got a theory. I just expressed an opinion.' But she agreed. It was the most solemn commitment they had ever made.

CHAPTER THREE

It was November. The decorations were already going up and everyone except the Iranian Government and the Mafia was recording a Christmas song somewhere.

Leonard and Gloria were shopping in the West End. It wasn't specifically Christmas shopping, but they were having a look round, just in case there was anything interesting about. It wasn't too busy; people were still a little nervous. It should have been obvious by now that Osama bin Laden was a one-trick pony and there would be no repeat of his murderous demarche. But some still wondered if it was safe.

Gloria wanted a party dress.

'Another dress? You've got more clothes than Marks and Spencer's.'

'If my collection was the same as theirs, I'd never go out.'

Then she added, 'I used to own twenty designer dresses but I gave them all to charity.'

'Oh, really,' said Leonard drily. He smiled indulgently at her.

'Are you hungry?' she asked.

'Ravenous. But we won't get in anywhere round here. Let's go to Islington. There's a lovely bistro there. I saw Simon Rattle in there once.'

'I hope you tipped him.'

'He was eating, not working there.'

This was vintage Leonard. He always treated other people's jokes as if they were irrational errors which needed correcting.

They thought it might be an adventure to get the bus, so they could look at London from the top deck. This was a mistake, and the journey took forever because of the traffic.

'Isn't this fun?' she said, kissing him.

'Most exciting. Next time we'll walk.'

'You wouldn't see the sights then. Unless you wore stilts.'

He put his arm around her and she snuggled up to him. Their romance had begun almost as soon as they had sat together on Shirley's sofa, and it had been facilitated by the proximity of their homes. Eventually they arrived at Islington.

'We could go and see Joe Orton's flat. It's just round the corner,' he said.

'Why? It's just a flat. He died years ago. Anyway, I thought you were starving.'

Leonard confirmed that he was, and they walked along Upper Street looking for the little bistro which seemed to have disappeared. Either that or he had made a mistake.

'Is this it?' she asked every time they passed an eating house of any kind. They found a likely place and went in.

'Yes, this is it,' he said as they took their coats off and sat down, but he didn't sound very sure. A waitress came up to their table and Gloria said,

'Has Mr Rattle been in?'

She shook her head and left the menus.

They studied the meals and Gloria said,

'I hope they do vegetarian.'

'Since when have you been a vegetarian?'
'Well...I am sometimes.'
In the end they both had linguini.
While they were waiting, she leaned forward and rested her chin on her hands.
'So, what do you think of me?'
'That's just what I was going to ask *you*.'
'Well?'
'I think we're both magnificent.'
She laughed and then said,
'Do you love me?'
'Well, I think it's a possibility.'
'I suppose I'll have to make do with that then.'
He leaned over and kissed her. Then he looked at the door and said,
'Bloody hell!'
Gloria was so startled she nearly pulled a muscle in her neck looking round. Shirley and Troy had just walked in. Although both couples had been seeing each other they had not communicated with the other two.
'This is embarrassing,' said Troy, shaking hands with Leonard.
'Why so?'
'Are we allowed to have dinner together before the five years is up?'
Shirley sat down and kissed Gloria.
'That wasn't the idea,' said Gloria. 'The idea was that we would see each other every five years even if we hadn't kept in touch.'
'How's tricks, matey?' said Leonard to Troy. Troy sat down and had to think about the answer to this.

'Good enough,' he said eventually. 'I'm going to see my agent tomorrow. I've been putting it off: I don't like cemeteries.'

'He's not in a cemetery, Troy. He has offices in London.'

'Yes, I must have been thinking of someone else,' said Troy drily.

They exchanged all their expectations and news; every forthcoming opportunity or hope suitably dressed up to sound as propitious as possible. Auditions were a dead cert, new plays a shoo-in for them. Every part they had heard about could have been written for them. It was just a question of walking in and claiming their rightful destiny.

'What about you, Shirley?' asked Gloria.

'I'm going for a musical, *Guys and Dolls*. Just down the road here at the King's Head.'

'Can you sing and dance?'

'Oh yes,' she said. Then she stood up and gave a short demonstration of her tap-dancing skills in the middle aisle of the bistro. Her flared red dress could have been deliberately selected for the routine. Her tap dancing was blistering and accurate but not subtle. Gloria tried to get up and join her, but Leonard pushed her back in her seat. The whole restaurant applauded wildly, and Shirley did an elegant curtsey before sitting again. Troy said,

'So that's the first actual show biz talent that you've told us about.'

'I can sing too!'

'Not here!' said Leonard, as if concerned about propriety. In fact, two displays of skills which he lacked would have been too much for him to bear.

'I'm amazing! Didn't I tell you?'

'So am I,' said Gloria.

'We all are,' said Leonard. They lifted their glasses and gave the Scottish toast.

'Here's tae us.'

'Wha's like us?'

'De'il th' ane.'

'And they're all deed.'

The waitress, who was Scottish and also a resting actress, gave it of her opinion that the English had enough to be going on with doing Shakespeare properly. There was enough conviviality to find this amusing.

After they had eaten, they chatted about this and that and the talk inevitably came round to the five-year meal. It was confirmed that they had meant every word of it. They should all keep in touch. What? Even if we split? Yes. Despite all outcomes. And every five years from September 11th as long as we are alive. It was all agreed.

CHAPTER FOUR

Troy was uncharacteristically ten minutes late for his appointment at the Narrow Escape Agency. That meant it was 12.10pm. There was no need to go all the way to the fifth floor: Percy Lillie, who handled his affairs, would already be drinking in the False Flag pub across the road. And there he was, sitting at a table and getting stuck into the lager. They shook hands.

Percy looked like one of those debauched spies who went straight from Cambridge University into Soviet intelligence in the thirties. A Bacchanalian *bon viveur* of mammoth proportions, his shirt front, tie and jacket lapels bore the traces of many an exotic luncheon. He had been born with a natural talent for consumption, especially of alcohol, and he had not neglected to develop it with constant practice. Percy pined for the good old days of entertainment when he and Oliver Reed had gone drinking together. (Actually, he was way too young to have known Reed, and wouldn't have lived this long if he had.) He was in a bad mood. Percy was always in a bad mood.

'Only bloody November,' he said, 'and the place is already filling up.'

Troy wasn't invited to sit down, but he sat anyway.

'Filling up?'

'Dilettante drinkers. Drive me up the wall. Never touch the stuff most of the year round. Then when it's Christmas you can't get a drink or a seat. And if you stand up then they tread on your toes. And you can't get to the bar either.'

He stopped himself with a long swig of lager while signalling at the same time with his eyes to the barmaid that he wanted another one. Percy was only forty, but the raspberry drinking blotches of broken vessels lit up his face like garish patterns on a Christmas jumper.

'Is that duffle coat new?' he asked Troy.

'No; I've had it for ages. There's no such thing as a new duffle coat. People get them from other people or have them for ages. What's wrong with it?'

'You look like a bloody sociologist.'

Percy peeled off a note and gave it to Troy who went to the bar and bought the drinks.

'Anything else?' said the barmaid.

'Yes, which sociologist do you think I look the most like?'

She stared at him. Perhaps she thought he was one of those dilettante Christmas drinkers who had one gin and tonic and thought they were Oscar Wilde.

Troy sat down again. Percy's first lager was now gone and he started greedily on the second. Another pint, and then he would move on to the top shelf.

'So, what's new then, Troy?' he asked.

'Nothing. That's why I came to see you. Is there anything?'

'Got a few things bubbling under. Nothing solid yet.'

This was not to be wondered at. Percy's life had far more to do with liquids than solids. But Troy said nothing. There was a long pause and then he said,

'Well, don't tell me. It's probably better that I don't know.'

Percy finished his second pint.

'I'll tell you as soon as I know for certain.'

'There are some musicals auditioning at the moment. A friend of mine has got a hearing.'

'I didn't know you could sing.'

'I can sing. A bit anyway. But you don't really need to sing for *Guys and Dolls*: Marlon Brando couldn't sing.'

'Some people think he couldn't act either, dear. But anyway, he was Marlon Brando. You can't do musicals, Troy.'

'Well, there must be something.'

'What about your voiceovers work? You've got another agency for that, haven't you?'

'Yes; they pay the bills, but it isn't what I went to RADA for.'

'No, of course not. You went to RADA to play *King Lear* at Stratford. Didn't we all? But I'm an agent now and you do adverts for corn plasters. Such is life, dear. We take what we can get and have to live with it. If I can, so can you.'

Troy was tempted to ask him if drink helped him be a man about the subject, but he kept silent again. He had spent his whole life keeping silent with people he needed.

After a pause, Percy said,

'There might be something.'

'Tell me. Did you forget the Globe had called about doing *Richard III* next summer?'

'No, they're still thinking about whether they want you or John Gielgud.'

'He's dead.'

'It's still a difficult choice. Have you seen *Herbert's Hotel*?'

Troy had never heard of it.

'It's a children's programme. Well, not exclusively for kids. More your sort of family type comedy. About a silly hotel in the wilds of…somewhere…'

'Oh, yes; I think I vaguely remember it.'

He had never seen it.

'You know the sort of thing. The hotel is chaos and all the guests are crazy. Well, they have this robot butler…'

'A what?'

'A robot butler. Apparently, he always goes wrong. Very popular character. Kids love him. The chap who plays him is leaving.'

All Troy could think of to ask was why a hotel would need a butler of any kind.

'Don't ask me. Lick up the honey and ask no questions.'

'This offer sounds more like dripping than honey.'

Percy signalled over his head to the barmaid with a mime representing pushing up a shorts glass into a whisky optic. It was good that all that dramatic training at Bretton Hall College hadn't gone to waste. He pointed to Troy's glass, but Troy didn't like drinking at lunchtime, so he shook his head.

'I was going to offer it to Jim Cathcart but he's not available.'

'Does the Globe want him instead?'

'No, he's got a film.'

'Your other clients do really well out of you.'

'I do a very good job for you, Troy, but it's horses for courses.'

'Well, try not to send me to the glue factory just yet. What happened to the old butler?'

'Booze,' said Percy, downing his scotch. 'It's a terrible thing. But he had the job for two series and it's good exposure. Public appearances and all that.'

Troy finished his beer which he hadn't really wanted.

'Go on. Put me forward. I'll try to watch it. Then I'll try to think of some ideas for developing the character.'

'You do that,' said Percy, who had no sense of irony. 'I'll tell them you can't wait. I think you'd be a first class Rumpledine.'

'Rumpledine? That's his name? Rumpledine?'

'Try and sound a bit more enthusiastic, dear.'

Troy leaned forward intently.

'Percy, *I want this.*'

'That's the spirit. I'll make a call. You were born to play it. And then you'll be a household name.'

'Percy, I've been with you for a year and I'm not even a household name in my own household. In fact, I don't even have a household. I can't afford one.'

'Your time will come, dear, you will be famous. But be a bit more enthusiastic.'

Troy did his intense pose again.

'Tell them I'll make them think differently about the part.'

'That's the boy. I'll be in touch,' he said, swallowing the last of his drink as Troy got up to go.

Troy watched the show that week. It wasn't too bad and sometimes it was quite funny.

A few days after his meeting he was called by Madge, Percy's colleague. Percy was off ill – something which happened more times than it didn't. She was calling about *Herbert's Hotel*.

'Sent them your showreel and CV, Troy. Absolutely loved it. They want to see you ASAP.'

'Great stuff.'

'Should keep you going for a while. How do you feel about it? Excited?'

Troy said what he said about every part he was offered.

'It certainly beats the bloody hell out of telesales.'

CHAPTER FIVE

It was the spring of 2002. The Americans were taking heavy vengeance in Afghanistan, and at home they were having quite understandable national hysterics. However, by this time, things in western Europe had grown calmer. Wild predictions about World War Three, made by America's numerous enemies in the British media, proved to be so much froth. Perhaps Shirley had been at least partly right.

Gloria had made her first steps towards superstardom by making a small appearance in a situation comedy on commercial TV called *Nobody Likes Bob*. She had played a girl whom the eponymous hero had met on a blind date. The scene had been well-written and Gloria shone through the small screen, as might have been expected. She had only been on for about ten minutes but had stolen the show. People had called up to ask who she was. Unfortunately, this was the last episode of the last series of the programme - but she had made her mark. She was poached by another, much bigger and more reputable agency. Her future, she was told, was assured.

Meanwhile the two romances continued.

'Where's Rumpledine?!' shouted Herbert Hickenlooper, the owner of *Herbert's Hotel*.

'He's in the cupboard!' shouted the children in the audience. They were filming at the BBC Theatre in Shepherd's Bush.

'Is he in the kitchen?'

'He's in the cupboard!'

'I know! I bet he's under the stairs.'

'He's in the cupboard!' they shouted.

'Or shall I look in the cupboard?'

The audience shrieked that he should most definitely look in the cupboard.

Troy, alias Rumpledine, was indeed in the cupboard. He was dressed as a butler, with a metal helmet and a battery pack across his chest like a domesticated cyberman. Troy liked being in the cupboard. He didn't want to come out and be seen by the world. He had a sophisticated girlfriend from a rich family. He wanted her to see him in *Endgame* by Samuel Beckett or *The Rivals* by Richard Brinsley Sheridan.

'Shall I open the cupboard, boys and girls?'

'Open the cupboard!' they shouted.

'Oh, Rumpledine! What are you doing in there?'

'I'm sorry, sir; I was just recharging my batteries.'

'No, you weren't. You were hiding from Mrs Hickenlooper because she wanted to give you some work.'

'She always wants to give me some work, sir.'

She should be my bloody agent, he thought.

'We always know where to find Rumpledine, don't we?'

'In the cupboard!' the children shouted.

After the show, Tom Sloane, who played Herbert, asked Troy if he was going for a drink afterwards.

'No, thanks. I'm going to go home and hide in the cupboard until next week.'

'Don't knock it, Troy. It's good, honest, regular work.'

'You missed out 'dignified'.'

'You can't have everything.'

'Well, that was Schopenhauer's opinion, anyway?'

CHAPTER SIX

You have got to be bloody joking, thought Troy, as he got to Shirley's flat. It was March now and they had been together for about six months. There was a note pinned to the door saying, *Troy, I had to go out. The key is under the mat. Help yourself to anything.*

The key is under the mat? Walthamstow Village was a nice area but – really? You have got to be bloody joking. He opened the door and went upstairs to the flat.

Help yourself to anything! The burglars round here obviously operated on an invitation-only basis. He turned on the TV, but that was the full extent of Shirley's absentee hospitality. As usual there was nothing in the fridge or the pantry. There never was. In their relationship, either they ordered food to go or went out to eat. On the rare occasions when they made meals at home, Troy bought the ingredients and cooked. He had learned to cook as a student, which is why they went out a lot. Shirley always offered to pay but he wouldn't hear of it. He was hungry now but what could he do? He had no idea when she would be back or where the hell she was.

He sat down in a chair and pulled a script out of his battered document bag. It was this week's episode of *Herbert's Hotel*. He was a minor celebrity now. People pointed at him in the street. He was semi-famous. A part-of-the-household name. Somewhere between the scullery and the servants' quarters. He wished he was dead. His clumsy black mobile phone rang. He tugged it out of his jacket pocket. It snagged on the edge and flew across the room. Luckily, it landed on the sofa and bounced instead of flying out of the window.

'Hello?'

'Hello, sweetness. It's me.'

'Where are you?'

'Don't panic. I'm on my way home. I'm about fifteen minutes away. Order a Chinese and I'll pay you when I get there.'

This wasn't an answer to his question, but he said,

'That's OK. I thought you were going to be here?'

But she was gone. The story of their lives together. A will o' the whisp: here one second and gone the next. And when she was there…

He used her landline to order the food.

Shirley had not been lying when she said that she was fifteen minutes away, but nevertheless she took over an hour to get home.

I'm here more than she is, thought Troy. But it was a nice place to be alone in. Better than his grimy bedsit. He transferred to the sofa and stretched out on the warm, yielding mock leather.

When Shirley eventually made an appearance, she was too busy to relax. She blew him a kiss and ran to put her stuff in the bedroom and also to remove a green creation which Troy thought was considerably more chic than a mere day-dress. The delivery girl came with the food at the same time. Her name was Soo. They were getting to be quite good friends. *She* was here more than Shirley as well.

When his elusive girlfriend emerged from the bedroom, she was wearing a blue leotard.

'You performing with the ballet tonight?'

'I need to practise my steps, loved one. I'm auditioning tomorrow.'

Troy wanted to ask her where she had been again, but he had to avoid sounding intrusive.

'You looked really nice just now. Anything special on?'

'Out and about. Meeting contacts - but I've got something special on tomorrow. They're doing *Guys and Dolls* and my agent's put me up for Miss Adelaide.'

'Well, that's fantastic. Where will it be? The Pontefract Boy's Brigade Hall?'

'No, silly. The King's Head in Islington. I told you.'

It had been ages ago that Shirley had said she had an audition for this particular show; yet it seemed that only now the project had come to fruition. That was a very common thing in show business. She sat down next to him and kissed him lightly on the nose as if he were a favourite nephew.

'Anyway, how's my little robot?'

A robot butler and a whirlwind, thought Troy. *It's a bad combination.* But he said,

'Well, I hope you get it. You should do. And if they ever do *The Tempest*, you should play Ariel.'

They went into the kitchen, got some plates and warmed them up under the grill. Shirley breathlessly explained what tap routine she was going to prepare. It was all he could do to stop her showing him while they were getting the food ready.

'Do you think I'll be magnificent?'

'I think you'll get heartburn if you don't slow down while you eat.'

They ate in silence for a while, which is to say that Troy was silent. After they had finished and cleared up, he managed to get her into the bedroom. It would do her less harm than dancing straight after a heavy meal.

Troy dozed off after they had made love. He dreamed that he was walking in a lovely wood out in the country. He could hear a woodpecker in the distance pecking at a tree. The knocking got louder and louder until he felt that the bird was right next to him. Then it seemed to be hammering at his skull. When he awoke, he realised that it was Shirley's tap routine he could hear. She was singing along to herself as she hammered the floorboards into submission.

I love you
A bushel and a peck
A bushel and a peck and a hug around the neck…
A hug around the neck and a barrel and a heap
A barrel and a heap and I'm talking in my sleep…
About you, dear…

After about only thirty minutes, she stopped and came back to bed, and they drifted into a restful sleep. When he awoke the next morning, she had already left. She had sellotaped a note to his head.

You looked so beautiful snoring, I just hadn't the heart to wake you up. Gosh, you toss and turn! I think you have more energy when you're asleep than when you're awake. Have lucky thoughts for me while I'm auditioning. Oodles of Love. Sh.

Underneath was a big red lipstick kiss. It was only when he went to the bathroom that he found there was another one on his forehead. He went back to bed but felt strangely restless.

A few days later, Troy was at Shirley's when his mobile rang. It was Leonard.
'Hello? Where are you? Are you with Shirley?'
'Yes, are you with Gloria?'
'Yes, we're getting married.'
'What…now? Can we come and watch?'
'No, not now, you div. We're sending you an invite. I just wanted to make sure you were still together.'
'We're still an item, if that's what you mean. Whether we're actually anything that could physically be called 'together' is a moot point.'
Leonard ignored anything he didn't understand.
'Gloria's here. I'll put her on.'
He passed the phone to Gloria. Troy congratulated her. They spoke for a few minutes and then he passed the phone to Shirley before she grabbed it. Shirley did a lot of the talking and he could hear Gloria doing most of the talking at her end too.
After they had said goodbye, Troy said,
'We can go to see that *Harry Potter* film tomorrow if you want.'
'Oh, my goodness – we can't. I'll be in Italy.'
'Italy!? What? I mean – why didn't you tell me?…What the hell is in Italy, for crying out loud?'
Shirley put her hand over his mouth.
'Calm down, darling! It's only a commercial.'

'A commercial? Well, I mean...that's great but...were you going to tell me?'

'I just did. These things happen very quickly.'

'No, I don't mean tell me as in a by-the-way afterthought as if I'm not important. I mean tell me as in loving communication, so that I know about things.'

'Troy, darling, I'm not emigrating. It'll only be for a couple of days. Well...four at the most.'

This conversation seemed to remind her that she hadn't packed anything yet, so she began running in and out of the bedroom with clothes and cases. Talking to her was like trying to catch a bird.

'This is the first time in ages I've had time off. Why Italy? Don't they have actresses in Italy?'

'They obviously want the best,' she shouted from the bedroom. 'I'm sorry...I thought you'd be happy for me. It's really good money.'

She came back in, sat down on the sofa and pulled on her knee boots. Troy assumed that either they were going out or *she* was going out.

'Well...I am happy. It's great. It was just a big surprise. I wish you'd communicate with me.'

She kissed him fully on the lips.

'Don't be silly. How can I communicate with you when I'm never here?'

There was no answer to such adorable insolence.

Shirley flew off to Rome early the next day. The television advert she would be filming was for luxury biscuits. She was met at the other end by a freelance British director called Danny Fonda. Danny was a sleek and smooth young geezer from South London. He was raring to go and had lots of energy, if not a great deal of finesse. But he looked competent and business-like. These adverts were good, short little earners for his private production company.

'Quick in, quick out and loads of bread,' he explained to Shirley.

'That's my philosophy too,' she said mischievously.

'Good stuff. I want to get this done today, lady, so no messing about.'

'I'm sure we can both handle that,' she said. She liked him and when she liked a man, she never saw any reason to keep it a secret.

Shirley - who had, of course, been late - was then rushed across town like the occupant of an ambulance to go immediately into make-up and wardrobe. The traffic in Rome was madness, as if everyone was late for an advertising shoot. Time was money on this job. Clearly this was not a British-style commercial with a blockbuster budget and all the time necessary to make a religious epic.

She went to wardrobe first and was given a beautiful evening gown to wear. Then, while she was being made up, Danny dropped in to go over her two lines and the requisite motivation. He was accompanied by a tanned, paunchy, bespectacled middle-aged Italian man dressed in a chic safari suit. He looked more like a film director than Danny. At least he looked like an *Italian* film director. He was introduced as Signor Lechesotti of the Lechesotti Biscuit Company.

'Don't get up,' said Danny. Shirley hadn't been about to get up.

Signor Lechesotti of the Lechesotti Biscuit Company was very pleased to meet Shirley. It wasn't often, he said, that you met British people who spoke other languages fluently. They often expect everyone to speak

English, he added. He rattled all this off in Italian. Shirley just stared at him. There was an awkward pause before Danny asked,

'Erm...Shirley, love, you *do* speak Italian, don't you? Your agent said you did.'

'Oh, yes, of course. But Signor Lechesotti speaks very quickly. And it's a regional dialect. I got the gist of it though.'

Signor Lechesotti of the Lechesotti Biscuit Company clearly had no English, so he could not be offended by the suggestion that he was some rustic yokel. Danny looked puzzled though. He had not thought of the Italian man as anything other than a sophisticated Roman. (And as he came from an Italian background himself and spoke the language, he should have known.)

'OK,' he said finally, 'as soon as you're ready we'll do a run-through.'

Actually, Shirley did know some Italian. She had taken GCSE Italian. She hadn't passed it, but she had taken it. She had been present in class when others had spoken it and she was a first-class mimic. She was more than accomplished enough to produce a convincing accent. Anyway, it was a Romance language, just like French. She had also taken French GCSE. She hadn't passed that either, but she knew Paris well.

She looked at the script. It was only a few words, as her agent had explained. There was a voiceover which some other actor did. She played the Contessa who liked rich, distinguished and delicious biscuits, as the narration would explain. Then she would taste one and say,

'Rich, distinguished and delicious – just like me!'

Or rather, she would say,

'Ricco, distinto e delizioso – proprio come me.'

Good grief, she thought, *you don't have to be Sophia Loren to cope with that. Should be a doddle.* Once she was dolled up and looking Contessa-like, she was taken down to the set.

The filming industry in Italy seemed to be the same as in England, with a ridiculous amount of over-manning. (Or more accurately, over womaning, since the place was crawling with pretty 'script girls'; one assistant for almost every male involved.)

Signor Lechesotti of the Lechesotti Biscuit Company thought Shirley looked like an angel and said so. He couldn't have been more delighted. She couldn't understand what he said but he was obviously well chuffed with the way she looked. He beamed happily with his face, his hands and his effusion of Roman eloquence. All was looking good.

'Right,' said Danny, 'let's have a little run-through.'

Shirley walked into the drawing room which had been built on the set. She took about thirteen seconds while an actor offset read the voiceover, the gist of which was basically,

Whenever the Contessa entertains her sophisticated guests for coffee, she always has a stock of these divinely delicious biscuits – and sometimes even when she is on her own!

Then the director signalled her to pick a biscuit out of the box and Shirley said, in a beautiful Italian accent,

'Ricco, distinto e delizioso – proprio come me!'

Then she tasted the biscuit. There was a pause. Then she grimaced like a troll.

'Eurghhh! Bloody hell!'

She spat the offending matter on the floor.

'Good grief! What are these made of? Baked Bean boxes?'

Signor Lechesotti was most offended and was also offended on behalf of the Lechesotti Biscuit Company. He began another effusion of less elegant Italian, with equal animation but less cadence than before.

'He says they've been making biscuits since 1800,' said Danny sharply. Signor Lechesotti of the Lechesotti Biscuit Company had clearly said a lot more than that.

'I believe him,' replied Shirley, swilling her mouth out with a hastily procured glass of water. 'Who did they make them for? The British Navy?'

It took a while to calm things down. Danny, with the luck of panic, decided to go for a quick take; and Shirley, no longer surprised by the rich, distinctive and sophisticated flavour of the biscuits, managed to pull it off.

Danny, whose Italian was near perfect, managed to communicate to Signor Lechesotti the ineffable vagaries of the Great British Sense of Humour. Naturally, Signor Lechesotti had heard all about it, just as English people had heard about Mussolini. No doubt the Italian entrepreneur would be assuaged by the quality of the advert when it was ready.

Shirley was not meant to fly back until the next day, so she had dinner with Danny. He was a handsome man with the charisma of endless confidence. She went back to his hotel room to have coffee with him. She stayed the night.

A jealous script-girl took her to the airport the next day. On arriving, she took Shirley's bags out of the boot and dumped them contemptuously on the ground.

'Just for future reference,' she said, 'you're supposed to sleep with the director *beforehand* in order to get the job. There's no need to afterwards.'

As she was Italian, Shirley could only be impressed by her grasp of the English language. The girl got back in the car and drove off. Shirley made her way into the departure lounge.

CHAPTER SEVEN

The wedding took place in July, 2002. It was a British summer, but they were lucky with the weather. Troy and Shirley arrived reasonably early. This was no less than a miracle of determined organisation on Troy's part since Shirley would have been late for the end of the world.

The marriage of Leonard Newton and Gloria Greatorex took place in a small local church in the wilds of Yorkshire, with the reception in a large country manor house within walking distance. Both sets of parents stood at the entrance to greet the guests. They presented a fascinating spectacle.

There was a lot of blonde in Gloria's heritage. It ran precipitously down both sides of the family and had collided with some force in the making of Gloria herself. Her parents were Thomas and Rhoda. Thomas, a solicitor, resembled the first Doctor Who, and looked as though he had his hair powdered by a Regency wigmaker. Rhoda, effulgent in white lace and chiffon dress, looked like a big-haired angel, as imagined by Country and Western singers in the Bible belt. Next to them were Leonard's parents, Melvin and Cora. They were both doctors and, like Leonard, were of surprisingly small stature, although neither of them evinced the compensatory force of personality which Leonard possessed.

Troy was particularly struck by an interesting anomaly. While Gloria had a very clipped, almost old-fashioned cut-glass accent, her parents both spoke with a clear Yorkshire brogue. On the other hand, the parents and relatives of Leonard – who had a very pronounced northern regional accent - were very well spoken upper middle-class people.

Everyone who was present must have been surprised by this inexplicable idiolectic contradiction on the part of their offspring. Not a few must have got the parents mixed up. Troy and Shirley exchanged their 'hellos' and 'yes-we-had-a-nice-journeys' and made their way into the ancient, elegant banqueting hall.

The room was a sight to behold, with dusty coats of arms on the wall and the occasional suit of armour to the sides. It wasn't the sort of place you wanted to rent out to the average English wedding party.

Guests filtered slowly in. Troy was shy and did not like approaching people to make conversation. Shirley, on the other hand, would make conversation with people without actually approaching them. He was glad when the room had filled up and absorbed the echoes of her spirited interrogations of complete strangers. Shirley was also adept at theatrical asides which could be heard at the back of the auditorium.

'My goodness! Look at that dishrag she's wearing! She must work in a charity shop.'

Eventually, Leonard and Gloria – she upstaging the angelic brightness of her mother in an outfit straight from an old Disney film – arrived to a rapturous round of applause and the revels commenced. The meal was sumptuous and passed without incident. The speeches did not stray from the routine expected and the jokes were received with warm and generous understanding.

After everyone had had their fill of food and personal anecdotes, they stood up and began to mix. There was a free bar, a dangerous gamble at a British wedding, but nobody seemed to be going too crazy and the atmosphere remained civilised. Troy began to mingle and finally wound up talking to Mr and Mrs Greatorex.

'Are you from London?' asked Rhoda.

'I live there, but I come from Nottingham originally. Not quite a northerner.'

Not quite a northerner, he thought. *Not quite an actor, not quite in a relationship.*

Actually, Troy's family life had been much more peripatetic than that, but he kept it simple. He was that rare thing: an actor who didn't want to tell you his entire life story. (Some of them will even leave it as a voice message.)

They all looked at Gloria as she swept past.

'She looks beautiful,' said Troy.

'Aye,' said Thomas glumly, 'that's the problem with weddings: everything's downhill from then on.'

Troy charitably assumed that his sadness arose from losing his daughter. They both kept talking but Troy wasn't listening. Out of the corner of his eye, he could see Shirley talking to Gloria's handsome brother Mark. Was it his imagination or was she flirting with him? She seemed to be touching his arm a lot. She was staring directly at him, and her feet were pointed directly towards him.

'Yes, yes,' he said to Rhoda, who seemed puzzled, since she hadn't asked him a Yes or No question. When Troy looked again, they, Mark and Shirley, had both disappeared. They seemed to have gone outside. He started to worry and made an excuse to Thomas and Rhoda. But while he was walking towards the exit, Shirley came back in on her own.

They had hardly had time to do anything illicit. Troy wondered if he wasn't being excessively sensitive.

As the evening approached, a tasteful French jazz band with a chic girl singer appeared and went through the standard repertoire of such bands. (*C'est si bon* and *La Mer* for starters.) All very nice and very French, with the pianist frantically going up and down the scale as if his hands were carrying out wartime evasion tactics.

After they had played and sung for about an hour, they had a small break. When they returned, they had a guest singer: it was Shirley. The band looked a bit uncertain about this. It wasn't that Shirley couldn't sing – she had a fine voice – but she hadn't been booked to sing and hadn't been invited to. The band's singer looked particularly unthrilled at being upstaged, if not by Shirley's voice, then by her red silk gown with a split going up to her neck. She didn't think of herself as a backing singer.

Shirley decided to sing *La Vie en Rose*. She turned to the band and said, 'Is that OK?' The band seemed bewildered and the singer looked as though she was about to spit fragments of glass, but they were professionals and rose to the occasion. All in all, it would have been a reasonable performance if Shirley had not forgotten the words halfway through. Luckily, most of the guests were well-oiled by this time and many might have thought it was part of a comedy routine.

When the song had finished, Shirley explained to the singer, whose name was Madeleine, that a professional would have joined in to cover the parts which she hadn't known. Madeleine looked at her like a mad basilisk, but as Shirley was too intimidating to confront, she said nothing. Leonard and Gloria looked at Troy as if he were Shirley's manager. Troy nodded and said, 'We have a problem, Houston.'

'Did you know about this, Troy?' asked Leonard.

'When did you last hear of Shirley either planning something or asking anyone's permission?'

Leonard turned to stare at Shirley and then shrugged off the incident.

After the band had finished their set which had been so impertinently interrupted, there was a disco with the obligatory embarrassing dancing, all of which would be preserved on video. Then the crowd of revellers stood back as Leonard and Gloria danced beautifully together to David Bowie's *The Wedding Song*. The rest of the night went spinningly well. But Troy seemed preoccupied and troubled.

Troy and Shirley did not really argue. Troy was too placid and Shirley would always be contrite and loving, although she never seemed to understand what her faults were supposed to have been. Troy was a sucker for her contrition because she never showed it to anyone else. Therefore, he took it as proof that she really loved him. And much as he hated to admit to excessive or obsessive passions, he really loved her.

The wedding incident was forgotten. And presumably, it had also been forgotten by Leonard and Gloria, since they were both invited to the opening night of Leonard's new *Hamlet* in August.

There is no exact term in England for 'off-Broadway'. Provincial meant out in the sticks; but this was in London, just not that part of London associated with commercial and artistic stardom. It was in the East End somewhere. Mile End way. They found it with some difficulty. The critics would also have difficulty finding it. Troy and Shirley went with Gloria. They met in the foyer. Gloria was very excited, as well she might be.

'I'm pregnant!' she whispered to Shirley. Shirley repeated the confidence in a voice which could be heard by the cast of *Cats* over in the West End. It was an exciting night for many reasons.

It was a small theatre – *Upstairs at the Star Inn, Hamlet tonight!* – but that has its compensations and is in many ways better. Firstly, you are more likely to get a full house, and even if you don't, a few people can make it look full. Secondly, it is more intimate. The actors can be seen and heard without artificial projection or hamming. Unfortunately, it also means that the audience can be heard by the actors. Tonight however, they were reasonably well-behaved. But Troy, Gloria and Shirley all agreed that this was a good place to start. With the wind in the right direction, the play could end up somewhere more consequential.

The trio took their seats and a man who forgot to introduce himself came onstage and announced that the programme was about to begin. When the curtain came up, it was obvious that the play appeared to be set in Denmark. The audience breathed a sigh of relief that it had not been updated to make a statement about patriarchal fascism in colonial Kenya or had not been set in a public toilet or a drag club.

The cast was a mixed bunch. Ophelia was quite good, but Polonius was played for cheap laughs. The ghost didn't have enough stage presence and probably wouldn't have been heard in a large theatre. Leonard was very good, but it wouldn't have been difficult to steal the show anyway. Troy and Gloria inspected the seating to see if they could see any famous faces, but it was too dark.

Gloria thought Leonard had missed the rhythm of the soliloquys – having put too much emphasis on researching the semantics of the speech. Shirley said he was brilliant. Gloria secretly hoped that Shirley wasn't going to get up on stage and help Leonard take his plaudits. The reception was greatly enthusiastic, and Leonard got two curtain calls. It was a triumph, but they wondered who would know it.

They all went backstage afterwards to offer their congratulations. It was a bit of a squeeze but they all got in. Leonard was in a buoyant mood, hugging and kissing both Shirley and Gloria. Troy said,

'Where's your smoking jacket?'

'I gave it to Larry, dear!' said Leonard in a fruity actor's voice, using a biro to mime a cigarette holder. There was much laughter. He was clearly jubilant.

Shirley had brought a bottle of that overpriced fizzy rubbish known as champagne. None of them drank very much, so a small bottle was more than enough. Nobody needed to be drunk. Everyone was happy. Shirley suggested dinner but Leonard explained that he was expected to eat with the cast, which they knew was the right thing to do. So, after more congratulations, hugs and kisses, Troy and Shirley left.

It was a short drive to Shirley's and she chatted excitedly about the night. She had Leonard halfway to the Baftas already. Troy thought it was nice that she was happy for him. The next day, they expected calls from Leonard and Gloria about the reviews. None came, so Troy called Leonard's mobile. Gloria answered it.

'Well,' he said, 'any notices?'

'None of the important papers were there – apart from the *Independent*.'

That isn't one of the important ones, thought Troy, but he didn't say so.
'Well, what did they say?'
'They liked Leonard, but they thought the production was a bit tatty.'
Shirley barged in with,
'That's great! If he rose above the play then that's good, isn't it?'
'Not if the play closes,' said Gloria. 'But we'll see.'
'But they liked Leonard. That's brilliant,' said Troy encouragingly. 'If it goes on, he's the star. If not, then he's got a great reference for his next role.'
'Yes, but who will know it?' she said, and they realised how disappointed she was. Neither of them dared ask where Leonard was or why he hadn't answered his own phone.
'Oh, cheer up,' said Shirley. 'It'll run for six months, I bet.'
Once they had said goodbye and hung up, Shirley's phone rang. Troy gathered from her hysterical eruptions that she had got the part of Miss Adelaide in *Guys and Dolls* at the King's Head.
About time too, he thought. The thing had been dragging on for months. But he was thrilled for her and they hugged and kissed. He managed to congratulate her before she crushed the breath out of him.
'Let's call them back!' she squealed.
'Er...maybe not just yet.'
'Why not?'
Troy was amazed that he had to explain to her that Gloria and Leonard weren't feeling too good at the moment.
'Well, this will cheer them up, won't it?'
'I don't think it works like that, darling.'

But they didn't have to call Gloria: she called them. She had got the part of Lady Macbeth in a new television film. She started rehearsals the following week.

'Oh, that is wonderful news!' said Shirley, almost interrupting to give Gloria her news as well. 'I bet Leonard is thrilled.'

'He's not here at the moment. He's feeling a bit down, so he's gone for a walk.'

'Well, he'll feel better when he knows about the film.'

'He already knows.'

Hamlet lasted four weeks, which was more than most expected.

The next few weeks were very busy for everybody - except Leonard, whose impressive triumph as Hamlet seemed to have impressed nobody who was in a position to offer him work. Gloria spent the next few weeks rehearsing and filming *Macbeth* for the BBC. Loose gowns were designed for her just in case production delays pushed the film into the third trimester of her pregnancy. Filming began later that year. Meanwhile, things began to move in other directions for Shirley. They had started in a small way with her agency sending her for a few voiceovers for radio. Her versatile voice and talent for mimicry led to her being offered voice jobs for cartoons and other lucrative work. This was a regular income – however, that was not something she had to worry about. The problem was that nobody saw her. A reputation amongst fellow professionals is one thing but being noticed by the public is much better. And in any case, Shirley was not one to be satisfied with not being seen or listened to.

'Can't you introduce me to your agent?' she asked Troy one night while they were at home.

'*My* agent? I'm looking for a new one myself. Mine's only got a couple of months before he's seeing snakes on the office floor.'

'Well, he got you on television, didn't he? That's what I want. I want people to actually see me and recognise me in the street.'

'Well, good grief, you're starring in a musical, aren't you?'

'When it eventually happens, yes. But that's only at the King's Head. It's not like *Cleopatra: The Movie*.'

'It's proper acting. You should think yourself lucky. You can be a household name by reading the news these days.'

Yes, but, I'm not the star.'

'Maybe we should swap agents. I don't want to be seen. Not when I'm a robot on a kids' programme.'

But Shirley told him he should be grateful that he was famous.

'Famous? I'm not famous. I'm on children's TV.'

'Somebody asked you for an autograph the other day, didn't he?'

'A ten-year-old boy with his mother. It's not exactly international notoriety, is it? I wanted to crawl under the pavement.'

Shirley told him he should know when he was well off, which he found irksome because that was precisely what she seemed not to know.

CHAPTER EIGHT

Macbeth was shown in late autumn of 2002 and it was a big hit. It had a brilliant cast and there was talk in the conservative press that the BBC had finally rediscovered its commitment to real public service broadcasting. The liberal media on the other hand, was excited into masturbatory frenzy by the fact that Macbeth had been played by a black man. The consensus was that Gloria had stolen the entire play, so everybody was happy. Except Leonard, who was 'resting' at the moment.

Gloria appeared on morning television to discuss the play and was all over the glossies modelling a new range of maternity dresses. She called Shirley and told her to watch the mid-morning women's programmes.

'Gloria Greatorex,' said the interviewer, 'fresh from her recent triumph as Lady Macbeth. I should imagine your phone is ringing off the hook at the moment.'

'Yes, Margie, I'm looking at plenty of offers now. By the way, if you live in London, please go and see my friend Shirley Gollancz at the King's Head in Islington. She'll be playing in *Guys and Dolls* and will be absolutely fabulous.'

Shirley squealed with delight and applauded the television set. Whether she was applauding Gloria or herself was a point on which Troy was not sure. But he had to leave for a rehearsal for the new series of *Herbert's Hotel*. He stood up to go but was stunned by Gloria's next announcement.

'I'm also appearing in the new production of Joe Orton's brilliant farce *What the Butler Saw* which will be on at the *Criterion* in the spring. I'll be playing Mrs Prentice, the wife of a lustful psychiatrist and my husband, Leonard Newton, the great Shakespearean actor, will be playing Dr Rance the investigator.'

Troy and Shirley were surprised by this. They knew that Gloria had been considered for the role but hadn't the slightest idea that Leonard had been signed up for the play.

'Leonard in a comedy?' said Troy.

'Don't you think he's a good choice?'

'Erm…I'm not even sure that he's been chosen.'

But if they were surprised, that was nothing compared with the reaction of Carl Brinker, the play's producer. He was straight onto Gloria after the show.

'Gloria! What are you up to? I didn't even know you'd accepted the role yet.'

'I haven't. I'm only offering to do it on condition that Leonard plays Dr Rance.'

'Don't be silly, darling! He's way too young.'

'What's that got to do with it? Good grief, this is acting we're doing, isn't it? What does his age matter?'

'But I had the comedian Bill McKinner lined up for it.'

'Oh Carl, you can't cast a comedian in a Joe Orton play. They'd ruin it by doing all their bits of business. They're characters manipulated by the plot. You have to let the lines do all the work.'

'That's true - but you do use *comedy actors*. Has Leonard done comedy before?'

'Has Bill done any theatre?'

They went back and forth like this for a while longer but eventually Carl had to give in. McKinner was a fading star and Gloria was as hot as hell. Plus, she had a point about never letting comedians near a Joe Orton play. So he agreed: Leonard was in as Dr. Rance.

Guys and Dolls finally got to the stage after a lifetime of delays. When Leonard and Gloria accompanied Troy to see it, it was a big occasion.

'One and a half celebrities,' said Leonard bitterly as the cameras took two snaps of his talented and beautiful wife for every one they took of Robot Troy. No-one asked Leonard to pose though.

Shirley was a great success. She had managed to make the part her own while paying tribute to the great Vivian Blaine, who had first played it on Broadway all those years ago. She had also insisted on putting a lot more tap dancing into the show.

Usually, when people say someone 'stole the show', they mean the opposite. They are usually referring to a star who accidentally stands out, by virtue of great talent or incandescent personality. When Shirley Gollancz stole the show, it was a deliberate smash and grab raid. She sang and danced beautifully, making all the songs and routines her own. Her personality, like her voice, went right to the back of the auditorium. But enough was not enough for Shirley and she began to ad lib, work the audience like a stand-up comic and generally turn the play into a one-woman show. This was no problem for the audience who were happy to have more than their money's worth. But it was far less than great news for the rest of the cast. Sky Masterson and Nathan Detroit found themselves supporting a supporting role. But that was show business.

When Troy, Gloria and Leonard went backstage afterwards, there were two and a half celebrities. Troy was pleased for them, but Leonard kept changing the subject of any conversation to the fact that he would shortly be 'starring' in the Orton farce.

Of course, before anything could be staged, Gloria had to have her baby, which arrived in February 2003. The media must have known that this was only seven months after her marriage, but they said nothing. It was a girl and they called her Melinda.

The next month, Britain and the United States moved into Iraq with all guns blazing to take out Saddam Hussain. The rights and wrongs of the invasion were hotly debated, but nobody really missed Hussain. Again, World War Three was predicted but failed to make an appearance. Panic came and subsided, and the world seemed to settle again.

As the year rolled on, life got a bit busy for Shirley. Troy would often arrive at her flat to find himself alone. He was a little worried that she might start charging him rent. Not because he was there so much but because she wasn't. She was becoming an absentee lover. Now this was hardly her fault: after all, she was a successful actress. She worked in the evenings and he worked during the day.

One Sunday he turned up at her flat, assuming that she would be at home, but she wasn't. He had a key but wasn't in the mood to sit around waiting for her. He was fed up with calling her to ask where she was. So, after sitting for a few minutes and debating whether to order yet another Chinese meal, he left and went back to his own unwelcoming place.

He got back to the depressingly dingy room about an hour later. He really needed to find somewhere else. He should have got himself organised before, but he spent so much time at Shirley's – and the assumption was always that at some time they would live together - that he had deferred the decision to get on the property ladder. A man in his position should have made this move a lot sooner. He fell asleep on the couch but was woken by his phone.

'Hello sweetie, it's me.'

'I came round. I thought what with it being Sunday, you would be in.'

'No; I had a lot to do. I went to see my mother.'

Troy had never met any of her relatives, which was odd given the length and intensity of their relationship and the fact that her family lived in London. (That was about the only thing he did know about them. For a voluble extrovert, she was strangely unforthcoming on the subject.)

'Shall I come over? It's still not too late.'

'No, not now. I'm exhausted. I'm going straight to bed.'

Troy thought that Shirley had never been exhausted in her life, but he said,

'All right, I'll see you tomorrow during the day. Once I've finished work, I'll come round.'

'All right, darling. Goodnight.'

They hung up. Troy began to think. Thoughts of buying himself a house lent some force to a germinal notion that he was at some kind of crossroads. He had been half living at the flat of a girlfriend who was constantly proving elusive. Should he buy a place or ask her to marry him? That itself was problematic. Shirley was a butterfly at best and a bouncing bomb at worst. Could he ever see himself married to her? Would she even say 'yes'? And yet – good grief – they were, to all intents and purposes, living together. But they never saw each other, just like a real married couple. They were like two statuettes in an Austrian clock, one coming out when the other went in.

He went into the bedroom and took off his jacket. As per his normal routine, he reached into the inside pocket to put his wallet on the bedside table. It wasn't there. He searched all his pockets. He did it methodically: he was not a man to panic. Think. Where did you take it out? Then he felt a flood of relief. He had taken it out at Shirley's because he had toyed with the idea of ordering a takeaway. He had put it on the coffee table; it must still be there. Shirley would keep it for him. No, that wouldn't do: he would need it tomorrow and he had an early start. He couldn't turn up at her flat at 6.00am; that would be bad form. He had to go tonight. He picked up his phone and called her again. No reply. He had to have the wallet, so he called a taxi and went over. He told the driver to wait for him as he had no cash with him. The driver was a little suspicious, but this was a nice area and Troy looked respectable, so he waited. This was very trusting of him, although he kept Troy's phone as security.

Troy let himself in and walked up the stairs. When he got to the main room, he could see his wallet on the table. He could see something else too: he saw a pair of man's shoes by the door. He walked softly over to the bedroom door and pushed it open.

Shirley was lying in bed. She was not alone. Whatever she and Mark Greatorex had done together was over and they were both now asleep. Troy wasn't sure what to do. He suspected that there was nothing *to* do. The taxi driver would be waiting outside with mounting impatience, so he went back downstairs and out of the door. On the way back, the driver talked and talked. They always do, especially when you have nothing to say back to them.

'I see you got your wallet,' she said the next day when he called her.

'Yes, I got it. And a lot more besides.'

There was a pause, so he said,

'Do you have anything to say?'

'No. There is nothing to say. I did what I did and I can't undo it. I don't love him but I did enjoy it. I'll probably do it again. The rest is up to you.'

'What was he doing down in London?' asked Troy finally. He knew he would never say a stupider thing in his life, so he added,

'I've still got some stuff there. Perhaps you could put it in a bag for me and leave it inside the door. When I pick it up, I'll leave my key.'

It was a few days before Troy got round to collecting the bag. It was the afternoon, so she hadn't left for the show yet. She was standing at the top of the stairs.

'I can't believe it,' he said. '*Now*, when I call, you're here.'

'I made a point of being here.'

She moved slowly down the stairs towards him.

'I'm sorry I said I wasn't sorry. I am sorry if I hurt you.'

Troy nodded and said,

'What if you hadn't been caught? Would you have been sorry then?'

He didn't stop to see her smile weakly and shrug.

CHAPTER NINE

The read-through for *What the Butler Saw* began a week later. The director, Carl Brinker, was there. Veteran comedy actor Timothy Bentham was cast in the role of Dr Prentice, the psychiatrist to whom Gloria played an alcoholic wife. A pretty newcomer, Alison Bolsover played Miss Barclay, the hapless secretary. Bentham, who was in his forties, must have been a bit surprised to find that the man playing Dr Rance, the elderly government inspector of asylums, was much younger than he was. But he said nothing; after all, he was the star, and he could hardly suggest that they swap roles.

After a cup of coffee and a chat, they sat round the table and began to read. It is usual for actors not to do too much in a read-through. It is better to let the characters develop organically rather than begin with them set in stone. Everything went quite smoothly until the surprise arrival of Dr Rance. Leonard gave him a grave, sonorous and lugubrious voice.

'Now let's not forget that this is a comedy,' said Brinker. 'Let's keep a sense of pace and a light touch.'

'This character is a madman,' said Leonard.

'Leonard's spent a huge amount of time studying Joe Orton's works,' said Gloria helpfully.

'Yes, I'm sure,' said Brinker. 'That's great. I'm a big believer in research and development...'

'Especially if you work in the electronics industry,' said Bentham.

'... and we always want to do something new, but...'

'...I recognise all the traits of a sociopath in this character,' insisted Leonard.

'Yes, but it is a comedy. We don't want to drag it down to destruction with a lot of character overkill.'

But Leonard was ready for him.

'Orton made it very clear that he didn't write fantasy. He always wanted them played realistically.'

The other actors leaned back in their chairs and looked at the ceiling. It was going to be a long morning. Bentham decided to help.

'I think that statement's been misunderstood, old chap. It doesn't mean that he wanted his plays to be like a funeral procession.'

'But that's exactly what *Loot* was.'

This was a reference to another of Orton's plays, in which the farce revolved around a coffin containing stolen money.

'Well, this isn't *Loot*,' said Brinker. 'And *What the Butler Saw* is a farce where characters are manipulated by the plot. Coincidence becomes the eternal and imprisoning destiny of man. They are caught in a tide of confusion and can't help themselves as they get swept away. The last thing they are is held down by gravity. It requires speed and pace to give it comedic momentum.'

This was so well phrased and delivered that the rest of the cast applauded it. It should have been decisive, and probably would have been with anyone other than Leonard Newton. They went back and forth until Gloria suggested that they just run through the script and see what happens. It was too early to start pinning anyone down just yet. This was wisdom too, so they carried on with the read-through. But it seemed like a long day. Leonard's use of long pauses and his deliberately saturnine delivery killed the comic pace which had been set up before his character's entrance.

They stopped for a break. Bentham collared Brinker for a quick chat.

'He's too young to play Dr Rance, you know old mate.'

This seemed like a good gambit on Bentham's part: just get rid of him altogether. Perhaps he wasn't aware of the politics involved.

'Are you offering to swap parts?' asked Brinker irritably.

'Good heavens, no. Otherwise it would be dead from the start. At least this way we'll know who's killing it, even if we do all have to go down together.'

Brinker gave a deep sigh and said,

'You understand the situation, don't you? If he goes, Gloria goes.'

'Bloody hell, man! She's famous but she's not Meryl Streep just yet.'

Bentham glanced at Gloria.

'She seems approachable: she's no prima donna. Perhaps she'll...you know...understand. I mean she's on the up but she doesn't own the studio, if you take my meaning.'

'No, that's not the way I want to play it. It's a challenge but I want him to see how to play the part properly.'

'Perhaps you could explain to him that a lunatic doesn't always have to be like King Lear.'

'I'll do my best. Look, Tim, it's only the first day. There's plenty of time to develop.'

And so, the reading continued. Brinker pleaded with Leonard to get a move on. The other actors could feel the strain of being held back in a play whose whole essence consists of animal spirits being unleashed. But the director never gave up.

'If it's madness you want, then release that manic craziness! We're not doing Harold Pinter here, for crying out loud!'

Leonard explained that he had not only studied Orton closely but had spoken with psychiatrists in his attempt to plumb the depths of the character's derangement. He knew he was right. While he persisted, Gloria, who took the view that her husband was a great actor, said nothing. She felt sure that he was bringing something to the role that the others had not seen, but which would have audiences and critics alike swooning with admiration. The rehearsals continued for a few days. Brinker and the others strained to get Leonard to unbend but without success. Eventually, Bentham shrugged and said,

'Well, it's a great play with some fabulous lines. Perhaps they'll carry us through.'

The rehearsals continued.

The play opened at the Criterion in May. Both Shirley and Troy attended, though not together. They saw each other in the foyer. Troy was alone, Shirley with a female friend. Their eyes met briefly, then they both turned away. This, for Shirley, was uncharacteristic diffidence, but she had been caught off guard and couldn't meet his gaze.

The play started well enough, just as the script-read had. The audience began to laugh as Bentham tried to seduce his new secretary. Then Gloria arrived and the chaos started to unfold. The audience were clearly enjoying themselves and the cast hoped that all would be well. Then Leonard as Dr Rance arrived. Made up to look like Dr Crippen seemingly, he walked slowly into the consulting room as if he had forgotten his lines. Then he began to speak with the kind of delivery that one would normally associate with an old Hammer horror film. It was like someone slamming on the brakes of a runaway bus. The play was suddenly drained of energy. All the laughs dried up. It bombed.

Troy left at the interval, mainly out of embarrassment for his friends, but also to avoid Shirley. But she had had the same idea. She was held back by no inhibitions and came straight up to him.

'What did you think?'

'Good grief, Shirley. What a question! It was appalling. Leonard seemed to think he was taking part in a day of mourning.'

'He will be tomorrow. Anyway, Gloria was very good.'

'Well, I hope it won't harm her career. But the cast is a team: if a play goes down, they all go down.'

Shirley looked round the foyer. Others had had the same idea and were leaving the theatre.

'Are you going backstage?' she asked.

'No, I don't think I could face them. I'm going home. I feel like I've just attended an inquest into a national disaster.'

'I'll give you a lift.'

'No, don't bother.'

He turned to go but she caught up with him.

'I made a mistake, Troy. You could always forgive me.'

He paused, wondering if she was sincere. Then he said, 'I'll think about it.'

The reviews came out the next day and the critics knew exactly whom to blame. Gloria was their darling and she received full exoneration. She was not even blamed for insisting that her husband be given the part. Bentham had been right: it had been quite obvious who was responsible, and at what point the play had collapsed. Everyone pointed out that Leonard was too young to play Dr Rance. It was interesting that from start to finish, nobody had noticed that Gloria was probably too young to play Mrs Prentice. Leonard became an infected brand. A more famous actor might have survived, but this had been his big chance and he had blown it. The critics, like all human beings, are merciless when they can get away with it. The only person who did not blame Leonard was Gloria. She still loved him and stood by him. If she saw a flaw in his argument that he was a genius, misunderstood by philistines, she did not mention it.

CHAPTER TEN

In late 2004, John Kerry tried to wrest the US presidency from George Bush. The pundits said that the American public would not 'change horses in the middle of a race', and for once they were right. UK Prime Minister Tony Blair dreamed of finding weapons of mass destruction in Iraq, but they all proved to be very well hidden, unlike Saddam Hussain, that poor country's recently dislodged dictator, who had been dug out of a hole the previous year and was now waiting for a judgment which could never entirely atone for his crimes.

Some people had even bigger challenges, like Shirley's agent, Rosa Tenthing. She was of a nervous disposition and had a particularly stressful job. The worst part of her duties was dealing with Shirley Gollancz. Not that she didn't like Shirley, and certainly not because she didn't rate her. Shirley was a hot property and deserved to be. But it was just well...challenging.

'There's no need to keep coming into the office,' Rosa told her. 'I can always call you if there's any exciting news. I'm sure there will be soon.' But Shirley kept right on coming into the office. Rosa didn't see why this was necessary, given that Shirley was fully occupied with *Guys and Dolls*, which was still running and in which she was a great success.

'Take her to lunch,' said Rosa's boss Marlene. 'That'll make her all nice and mellow.'

'You mean it'll get her out of the office, so you don't have to talk to her,' said Rosa.

'I don't mean any such thing,' said Marlene, 'but she's your client. You took a chance on her and she came up trumps. I wouldn't dream of poaching her.'

'And now I'm stuck with her.'

'What are you complaining about? She's a goldmine for you.'

'She'll dance in the restaurant,' said Rosa sulkily.

'Well, there we are then. Most people would have to pay to see that.'

'She doesn't drink but she behaves like a drunk.'

But they could already hear Shirley coming up the stairs like the Queen Mary coming into port.

'Shirley darling!! Hello! Rosa is all ready for you!' said Marlene as she whisked past her to go out. They kissed briefly in passing and then Marlene disappeared. Rosa also hugged and kissed Shirley.

'I've got a lovely lunch booked in this gorgeous little place,' said Rosa. 'It really is very *quiet* so we can have a nice *quiet* chat. I always think it's the best place in London to have a *quiet* chat.'

They made their way downstairs and flagged a taxi. Rosa's quiet little place was the usual box-sized Italian bistro hidden away in the back streets of the West End. The waiter knew nothing about a booking but found them a table anyway. He gave them menus and Shirley ordered something that wasn't on it. There was an argument which had to be resolved by the manager. Rosa, thinking to simplify things said, 'I'll have what you're having'. This meant that the chef had to make two specials instead of one, which caused more trouble. After they had settled down, Rosa said,

'So how is *Guys and Dolls*?'

'Great! You've seen it haven't you?'

'Well, of course! But not every night. Still going all right?'

Oh yes. Great. Marvellous.'

'Good, well, that'll keep you off the streets for a while. Erm...was there anything you wanted to talk about in particular?'

The drinks arrived. Shirley had fizzy water. Rosa took a big gulp of her fortifying wine.

'I've heard that they're doing a film about that Diana Forella.'

Rosa smiled and looked interested. There was a pause. Shirley continued,

'The American stuntwoman.'

'Oh, great. Are you hoping to get a part in it?'

'Well, yes: I want to play Diana Forella.'

Rosa seemed surprised by this.

'Well, I should think that they are probably going to cast an American actress.'

'I can do a perfect American accent. I'm doing one every night. I can do every accent there is.'

'I'm sure you can, but...'

Rosa did not have time to point out that Miss Adelaide's accent was not quite that of every American. Besides, it wasn't really the point - and Shirley was a first-class mimic. Rosa knew where this was going and had to head her off somehow.

'See if you can get me in. I really want this, and I could do it standing on my head.'

'It's not a question of that. It's a more delicate question of...national sensitivities. A British woman playing such an iconic American heroine...they really don't like that sort of thing.'

'But Renee Zellweger played Bridget Jones.'

'Erm...yes...'

Rosa was quite surprised that Shirley couldn't see that the argument didn't travel both ways. American money would dictate who played what. And furthermore, if Miss Zellweger's British accent hadn't been flawlessly perfect, there would have been riots on the streets of London.

'Anyway, haven't they already got someone...?'

'No, they haven't. It's still in the planning stage.'

Rosa was greatly relieved to hear this.

'Well, that's fine. I'll keep my ears open for...'

The food arrived and Rosa thought that this was the moment to change the subject.

'Now let's talk about your next project...'

'This is my next project. I've told you I want to play Diana Forella.'

Rosa knew that distraction had failed. She had to take the direct approach.

'I don't think it's going to be possible, Shirley.'

'Diana Forella spent her last years in England. She died in Croydon. I know that they're coming over for the auditions. That's what it says in *The Stage*. The director is going to be David Hoffman. He directed that film *AutoSlaughter*.'

'Yes, I saw it. It was rubbish.'

'It was a smash hit and made trillions. Put me up for it, Rosa.'

Rosa decided to withdraw to a more defensible position.

'Well, all right, I'll put you up for it. Now tell me what experience you have in stunt work?'

'Good grief! I won't have to do the stunts myself. It's only a film. They'll have stunt women for that.'

'That sounds like quite an irony, doesn't it? You know, using stunt women for the stunts of a stunt woman.'

'Vivien Leigh!'

'Pardon me?'

'Vivien Leigh was a British actress who played an American. Mention that when you call him. Call him now.'

'Who? What? Shirley, we're having lunch. As soon as I get back to the office – I mean, I don't even have his number...'

'I have. At least I've got his office number. Call him now.'

They argued for a bit until Rosa realised that Shirley wasn't going to let it go away. She took the number and called the office of David Hoffman. It would be 8.00am in New York so she would probably have to call back later anyway, which would have been excellent. But David Hoffman was one of those workaholics who get into the office before his staff. He actually answered the phone.

'Hoffman.'

'Oh, hello, Mr Hoffman. It's Rosa Tenthing from the YBC agency in London. I'm calling about the new film about Diana Fortella.'

'Forella.'

'Yes, Forella. Well, I'm lunching with my hottest actress, Shirley Gollancz, who is currently starring in *Guys and Dolls* in the West End...You have?...Oh, my goodness.'

Rosa mouthed *He's seen it* across the table.

'Well, I'm sure she'll be thrilled to hear that.'

He loved you! she mouthed again.

Then there was a long pause as Rosa did more listening than Shirley thought appropriate.

'Ah, yes, I see. Well, that certainly makes sense...yes, well, thank you so much for talking to me, Mr Hoffman.'

She clicked off the phone, apparently to Shirley's mystification.

'Well?' she demanded. 'What did he say?'

Clearly the early termination of the call was an act of treachery and cowardice.

'It turns out that we were wrong. They want to use a real stunt woman for the picture. They think it would be ridiculous otherwise.'

'And?...'

'And?...Well, Shirley, you're not a stunt woman,' offered Rosa weakly.

'How the hell do you know what I can and can't do?

The other diners were taking an interest in the proceedings. Rosa tried lowering her voice in the time-tested and eternally useless method of trying to make someone else speak more quietly.

'I'm your agent, Shirley. I know you aren't a stunt woman. There's nothing on your CV about it.'

'Oh, for goodness sake,' bellowed Shirley, 'how much brains and talent does it take to fall off a bloody horse? Call him back.'

'Shirley, I can't call him back.'

There was a heavy silence in the restaurant. The place was turning out to be quieter than Rosa had expected. She looked round. The customers and the waiter looked back at her. They wanted to know why she could not call him back.

'*I'll* call him,' said Shirley. She grabbed Rosa's phone and pressed the redial.

'Honestly, Rosa – who uses four ones for a pin number?...Mr Hoffman? My name is Shirley Gollancz. You just spoke to my agent...Yes, why thank you!...Yes, we do love that show and we're very glad you were able to see it while you were over here...You're kidding me?...Well, that's fantastic!...We'll be able to meet when you come over...Oh good heavens, I've done all sorts!...I can fall off a horse, drive a motorcycle over a cliff...you name it really...'

And so on. Rosa was speechless. Hoffman was coming over in a few months and he had agreed to meet her. Shirley handed the phone back to her agent.

'And that, my dear, is how it's done.'

Rosa was impressed. So were the customers, who applauded wildly.

CHAPTER ELEVEN

Gloria didn't have to pester anyone. Her agent was, at least for now, a mere order taker. The offers flowed in over the phone and it was only a matter of time before Hollywood became interested. A film part in America soon came her way.

It was 2005 and Melinda was two now. She could either travel with her mother to the US or stay with her father – who currently had very little to do - in the UK. Or they could all go. This last option would be the best. But Leonard had not yet given up hope of landing an important role, and he enjoyed being a father, so he decided to stay.

Gloria had flown over for initial talks and then returned. The film was based on a book which was based on the life of someone long forgotten. But it had a lot of money behind it. It would likely be the big hit of whichever year it was released.

Before she left, Troy made a visit to their surprisingly modest house in Streatham. They were both happy to see him. He was glad to see them. Gloria was as radiant as ever. There was nothing in her manner to suggest that fame would spoil her. She looked super glamorous in just a baggy jumper and ski-pants. Little Melinda was running about in a romper dress. She stared at the visitor in bewilderment for a few seconds. Then she pointed at him.

'He's a man,' she said.

'Well, that's debatable,' said Leonard which caused much amusement. They drank coffee in the spacious lounge while Melinda went round the room either pointing at things or hitting them with a yellow plastic

hammer as the mood took her. She sang a song while she was doing it. After a while, Gloria said, 'Shirley was here last week.'
'Oh yes.'
'Yes, that was an unfortunate incident,' said Leonard.
'We thought you would marry.'
'Erm...I don't think it was ever that certain.'
'You were so well suited,' said Gloria.
'Oh, good grief! Well suited? We were well suited like George Bush and Vanessa Redgrave. We had almost nothing in common.'
They realised that he didn't want to go any further on the subject, and Troy didn't want his personal life to spoil the occasion, so he said,
'Tell me about this film then, Gloria.'
'Well, it's a sort of action romance biopic sort of thing... Routine stuff. The script arrived yesterday. I think it needs a bit of work.'
'It's garbage,' said Leonard.
Melinda concurred with this diagnosis. 'It's garbage,' she said.
'It's not garbage, darling. It just needs a bit more filling out.'
'I'll rewrite it,' said Leonard. 'Won't I, Melinda? Say 'garbage'.'
'Daddy, the script is garbage.'
His daughter came over and sat with him. She was asleep in an instant.
'Looks like the sky's the limit for you at the moment, Gloria.'
'Well, you're a household name, Troy.'
'I certainly am. But I had a bit more in mind than playing a robot when I went to RADA. Well, I suppose it keeps me out of snuff movies, or worse, telesales. And I can take stock. Be a bit more choosy about offers. Assuming I get any.'

'Consider yourself lucky, mate,' said Leonard.

'Well, I do, but you know this business: it comes and goes. Our situations could be reversed next week.'

'Let's hope so.'

'Thanks.'

'He didn't mean it like that,' said Gloria.

'I wouldn't mind being a robot for a few weeks if you're fed up with it.'

Troy could just imagine Leonard developing the role by researching cybernetics and the history of domestic service. The thought amused him; not much amused him these days. He had become strangely reflective. As for the current situation, it was difficult to know what to talk about. If he stressed Gloria's success, it would embarrass Leonard, although he felt sure that he was happy for his wife's success. Leonard had nothing to talk about. And he, Troy, didn't want to talk about Shirley. That left only Melinda and he could only say how cute she was so many times. But they were friends so there was no awkwardness. They could talk about nothing without feeling that time was being wasted. He stayed for about another hour and they played a good-natured game of Scrabble. Then Troy said he had to go.

'How long will you be away?' he asked Gloria.

'About a month on and off. I won't be staying there.'

'Well, I'll see you when you get back.'

Troy got up to leave. He shook hands with Leonard, who didn't want to get up for fear of waking the little girl. Gloria saw him to the door. They hugged and he said,

'Everything OK with you two?'

'Yes, it's all great. He's a little sluggish but that will pass, I'm sure. He needs some work. He's been talking about doing some writing.'

'Don't let him near the script.'

She smiled and opened the door for him.

'I won't. Although he's right: it is rubbish.'

'Good. Should be a smash hit: there's a huge market for rubbish. I should know; I've been in enough. Take care.'

As he walked down the long gravel drive, she said,

'Troy, it's none of my business…'

'Is this about Shirley? That was ages ago.'

'I think she's interested in…'

'Oh no. That's definitely over. You can feed that back to her if you want. I'm well over it.'

'I can see you're not - and I don't think she is either.'

'Please don't get involved, Gloria.'

'I have to. I feel so guilty because it was my brother. I could have killed him when I found out. He's always been something of a cad.'

'Are you saying I shouldn't blame her?'

'Well, maybe not entirely.'

'Thanks, I'll try to put that idea to some use. Anyway, it was a long time ago. We both ought to move on. And I'm sure *she* will have.'

There was a pause. Then she nodded, blew him a kiss and closed the door.

CHAPTER TWELVE

As the date approached when Hoffman would be in England, Rosa called with instructions. Shirley was a bit suspicious that the meeting was in a hotel room; but she duly arrived at the Tower Hill and went to room 1406. She knocked, and a short, stout, bald American man wearing an iridescent kimono answered the door.
'I was supposed to meet a Mr Hayward,' she said.
'Yes, that is I,' said the man. The grammar of educated Americans is always better than that of British people. 'Come on in.'
Shirley hesitated.
'Don't worry,' he said. 'My wife is here.'
The man nodded his head towards the big double bed. His wife was not up yet. It was 11.00am. What happened next was so shocking that Shirley didn't realise that it saved her by giving the game away. The man's wife smiled at Shirley, pulled back the covers and patted the space next to her. She was completely naked. His wife, if it was his wife, had jumped the gun before Shirley had entered the room.
'Goodbye,' she said, running off. Shirley was not a crier, but she came close this time. She felt disgusted, dirty and somehow – although it made no sense – cheap.
Once she was back in her flat, she called Rosa and bawled her out. Rosa was almost in tears too.
'I know nothing about this. I thought the meeting was with Hoffman.'
Rosa felt herself the victim of an injustice: after all, it was Shirley who had made this appointment. After she had calmed her down, she said, 'Leave it to me. I'll find out what's going on and call you back.'

Shirley paced about the flat, seething with humiliation and muttering to herself. She was not good with humiliation. Eventually, Rosa called back.

'The man was called Hayward.'

'I know that much.'

'He's an agent for American film companies in the UK. He's used to make preliminary interviews. He screens and vets everyone. You can guess why.'

'Screens and vets!' bawled Shirley. 'Did anyone screen and vet *him*?'

'I've spoken to Mr Hoffman. He will call you personally in ten minutes.'

'Yeah, I bet.'

'Oh, he will. I guarantee it. He won't want this to get out.'

Shirley hung up and waited. After fifteen minutes, she thought, *I knew it*. But she didn't know it. After twenty minutes, Hoffman was on the phone. He was profuse and abject in his apologies and promised to look into it.

'I don't know what the hell is going on here, but I'll find out,' he said decisively.

'Did you speak to Hayward?'

'Sure. He says it was all a mistake and a joke. But he sounded scared stiff. They're going back to the States this afternoon.'

'Was the offer of a film part genuine? Or do I have to pass the casting couch audition?'

'No, it was totally genuine. I've seen your resume. I've seen you in *Guys and Dolls*. Very impressive. I'm sold on you. Let's meet - I mean properly this time.'

'Somewhere public.'

They arranged an encounter in the lobby of Hoffman's hotel in the centre of London. After she had thanked him and hung up, she said, 'Right, we'll try again.'

This time when she arrived at the hotel, she was shown into the lounge. Hoffman was chaperoned by a middle-aged female assistant, who made an excuse and left them. He motioned her to sit with him in one of the plush chairs.

Hoffman was a typical up and coming film director. He was tall, strong-looking, firm in his handshake and confident; a confidence which arose naturally from his dark good looks. He gave off a sense of energy even when motionless. Shirley wasn't sure how old he was. Probably too old to be a boy wonder, but not so old that this film was his last chance. They ordered coffee and he took out his laptop to call up her CV. He re-read it briefly to refresh his memory and said,

'There's some impressive stuff here. I hope it's not too good to be true.'

'Thanks. I think you'll find it's all in order.'

He narrowed his eyes.

'You really can do all these things, can't you? It's just that my people said they've never heard of you. I don't mean as an actress - of course, we know your reputation there. But as a stunt performer...'

'Well, I always say, if you've fallen off one horse, you've fallen off them all.'

She smiled and he smiled back at her. Then he added,

'If you can, then I'd like you for the part. Of course, the suits will demand someone better known in the States, but I can handle them if everything else is OK. And you look a lot like Forella.'

'Pretty, was she?'

'Oh, yeah.'

They smiled at each other again. He had a dangerous smile, not a nice guy smile. This was a man who could charm and destroy in the same breath.

Hoffman explained,

'We're in an unusual situation with this picture; we want a stuntwoman to be the star. But that means we can't use someone who is world famous. Firstly, there are no big stars who can do these things. And secondly...'

'Insurance,' said Shirley, to prove she was listening.

'Exactly. The money wouldn't let a big star do these things. Of course, if the picture is a success, you'll *be* a big star.'

'And then *I'll* be uninsurable.'

'But then you can pick your parts. But for now...we need to get this one right. I'm going back to New York Friday. Are you OK to come back with me?'

'Of course.'

They finished their coffees and chatted about the film. She left about 1.00pm but they arranged to have dinner that evening. Naturally.

CHAPTER THIRTEEN

Films are huge operations, and it often takes a commensurately huge amount of time to get them off the ground. Sometimes negotiations can go on for years with the film never getting made. It has been known to take ten years just to get a script finalised. Not surprisingly, it was many months before Shirley actually heard that the film would go ahead. She and Hoffman were an item by this time so there was no need to spend time kicking around in hotels. He was free after his second divorce, so whenever she flew over, she could stay at his sumptuous house in Chappaqua, New York State. They had experienced a lot of waiting and were both keen to get down to the work.

Shirley had asked to see the script and was surprised to find that there wasn't one. The script was being written – or rather re-written - and was currently in what was known in Hollywood as 'development hell'. This meant that a talented writer had produced an original and witty screenplay which was now being pulled to bits by ignorant executives who shouldn't have been trusted to compile a shopping list. But she did have a rough synopsis.

Diana Forella was one of those people nobody had heard of until she died in 1996. She had been a stuntwoman during the 1970s. This was the heyday of the great disaster movies, which had been designed to get people off their TV couches and into the cinemas by making films which people just *had* to go and see. At this stage, the script wasn't necessary for Shirley because she hadn't been offered the part yet. Her acting skills were not in doubt, but she had to prove her abilities in the field of rodeo and motorcycles. These were skills which she had claimed on her CV – a confused document in a permanently protean state.

For this purpose, they went to upstate New York. It was hardly cowboy country, but they wanted to be out in the wilds, so they drove to a deserted brick shack, which did service as an office, next to a gravel and grass circuit plus stables. There was also a couple of motorcycles, ready for daring deeds to be done on them. A small, wiry, leathery man with a deep southern drawl came up to meet them. He was wearing a baseball cap and an eyepatch. He introduced himself as Roddy. They shook hands and he asked Shirley if she was ready to try something.

'Of course,' she said. And then, being Shirley, she pointed to his eyepatch and said,

'Is that from doing stunts?'

'No; my ex-wife poked it out with a pencil.'

Hoffman left them to get acquainted. He went into the shack to make some calls and check his emails.

'Come on,' said Roddy, 'I'll show you around.'

As they walked towards the stables, he turned to her and said,

'Rule number one: contrary to what many people think, we stunt professionals like to live as long as possible. We like to stay healthy and in one piece. Now being a stunt professional yourself, you'll know that.'

Shirley nodded.

'In fact,' he continued, 'we're all downright cowardly 'bout the whole thing. We like to do as little damage to ourselves as we can.'

'Same here.'

'We're not like British rock drummers,' he added, on a cultural note. Shirley gave a tight smile and nodded as if she were thinking the same thing. They reached the stables.

'What have you ridden in England?'

'Oh, all sorts.' She managed not to shrug, but Roddy looked suspicious nonetheless.

'We'll start with Brandy,' he said. He gave her a crash helmet and some kneepads which she put on. Roddy fetched out the eponymous nag. Brandy was a cartoon horse who was one step away from being stuffed. 'Try her.'

Shirley mounted the nag. To Roddy's relief, she had obviously ridden horses before. She took the decrepit mare on a canter round the circuit. When she had returned and dismounted, he said,

'OK. You can ride, but that's only the beginning. Let's try Joey.'

Joey was a younger male brown horse. He was a bit more spirited. Shirley mounted him and he seemed to resent her a little at first. But she managed to get the upper hand. She took him on a gallop round the circuit.

'Good,' said Roddy, when she had returned. 'Now take him round again. But do something fancy. Make out you're the Lone Ranger.'

Shirley took Joey round at a livelier clip. This time, on passing Roddy, she dismounted while the horse was still running. He was impressed, but also a bit worried.

'That was very good – for a first attempt. You never done that before. I can tell.'

Never try and fool a pro.

'Well, I've done it now, so it should be easier the next time.'

They spent another half hour with the horses. At the end of the session, Hoffman came out of the shack to check on her progress.

'How's it going?'

Roddy took him to one side and talked to him for a while. It wasn't difficult for Shirley to guess what they were saying. It was clear that while Shirley had ridden before, she had no stunt training. Roddy could recognise when there was a practised technique being used. Hoffman replied, 'What I figured. Do you think she can do it?'

'Maybe. I don't know enough yet. We'll try a spin on the bike before we get to jumping off burning buildings.'

Hoffman looked at Shirley and smiled. Then he said to Roddy,

'I really want her for this part if she can do it. But don't tax her if you think she can't. I want her in one piece at the end of it.'

'Sure.'

The director looked searchingly at Shirley for a few seconds, then went back inside. Roddy went back to Shirley and asked her if she wanted coffee.

'Not yet. I'd like to press on.'

'Now you have ridden bikes before, haven't you, Miss Gollancz?'

'Of course.'

'Let's have a try. And don't do anything spectacular yet. I just want you to get used to it.'

'Understood.'

Roddy had lain both of the bikes on their sides. He wanted to see if Shirley knew enough about them to lift them up properly. (There is a particular technique.) She did. So far, so good. She mounted it, started it up and took it round the circuit. Again, it was obvious that she had ridden one. But she had guessed at the content of their conversation. They were beginning to suspect that she had exaggerated her skills. She knew she had to do something daring. Better to do it on a motorbike, she reasoned, which is the devil you know, rather than a horse, which can be unpredictable. She took off again before Roddy could get to her, taking the circuits faster and faster. Roddy tried to motion to her to pull in, but she ignored him.

Once she had a feel for the machine – it was slightly more powerful than her brother's bike, the only one she had ever ridden before – she decided to go for broke. On the fourth circuit, she gunned the bike up to get maximum momentum before trying the same precarious move that she had performed on the horse. In other words, she tried to dismount while it was still going. Perhaps she had assumed that Americans in the film industry wouldn't be too concerned about the cost of the machine. One of her safety kneepads caught on the side of the bike as she tried to jump off. She pulled the bike off-balance but couldn't escape as it crashed into the shack with her attached to it. The hut was made of brick and stone. She died instantly.

Troy's phone went off at 3.00am. No phone call that comes through at 3.00am is ever going to be good news. It was Leonard.
'Mate...Wake up. This is awful and I don't know how to make it better than it is.'

He told him what had happened. Troy felt paralysed for a moment. After a few seconds, he pulled himself up and sat on the edge of the bed. It took a lot of effort; he felt about ninety. Leonard didn't have much to add except,

'Call me if you need me. Don't call Gloria: she's in a bit of a state.'
Leonard paused and then said, 'Are you still there, mate?'
'Yes. Yes, I'm still here.'
Leonard said, 'OK' and rang off.
Troy sat for a moment and then ran to the bathroom to be sick. Then he came back and sat on the edge of the bed again. He was still sitting there when it got light.

The funeral took place at Golders Green crematorium. Troy was in a daze as he tried to find it. He asked two middle-aged Jewish men where it was and then stepped into the road before they could tell him.
'Yeah, that's right,' said one of them, pulling him out of the way of an oncoming lorry. 'That's the best way to get there.'
He met Gloria and Leonard outside, but they were all too choked with grief to say anything. They just hugged and cried. Melinda wasn't with them.
As is often the case with funerals, they thought they would be able to bear it until the coffin came in. Then it was too much, and they broke down again. The ceremony was kept simple. Clearly, nobody was in the mood to dwell on the loss.
Afterwards, they went back to the family home. It seemed amazing to all three of them that they knew so little about her family. Troy had been in a relationship with her and had never even met them.

The Gollancz residence was a big place in Hampstead. The family made them quietly welcome with as much friendly hospitality as grief can allow. Troy was introduced to a man of about fifty. He gave his name simply as Jason. He got the impression that the man had been just as desolate as he seemed even before the tragedy, as if this were the last in a long series of defeats. Those defeats were clearly not financial, but they were there in the man's eyes. He seemed broken beyond any recovery.

'My name is Troy. I was a close friend of Shirley's. I'm so sorry.'

He didn't say anything about their relationship.

'Thank you for coming,' said the man slowly. He didn't introduce himself any further than his first name, but Troy assumed that he was Shirley's father, although there were a great many other relatives present. The man shook his hand absent-mindedly with his sad, moist eyes fixed on some distant point.

'Such a waste,' he said finally.

'Yes, a tragic waste,' said Troy.

'We had such plans for her.'

Troy paused to measure his words and then said very softly, so as not to sound inappropriately contentious,

'Shirley didn't strike me as the sort of woman other people made plans for.'

'No, that's true. But there are ways of making people follow their own interests. It's what life is all about.'

Again, Troy weighed his words carefully and asked, as if it were a casual point of interest, 'What would you describe as her interests?'

The man became a bit vague on this question. He started to say something about the success that could have been hers, but his voice tailed off with exhaustion born of inconsolable emptiness. After a while, Troy placed his hand on the man's shoulder and said, 'God bless you'. The man nodded but Troy could see that he wasn't really there.

He went and sat on a sofa next to a venerable female ancestor with snowy white hair. She looked like a survivor from some lost, legendary people. In a sense, she was. She turned and looked at him for a few seconds. Then in a central European accent which he could not place, she said, 'Are you an actor?'

He nodded and then said, 'I knew her well.'

'You lost your friend.'

'I lost her twice,' he replied.

The old woman nodded herself and then turned away. Then she said, more to herself than to Troy, 'A motorcycle she died on. Doing tricks on a bike. For this, you send children to college.'

CHAPTER FOURTEEN

Leonard and Gloria kept in touch with Troy over the next few months, their friendship reconfirmed by the tragedy. There was the occasional visit. Congratulations for newspaper stories of success were posted on Facebook. There weren't too many of these and they were mostly for Gloria, who continued to go from strength to strength.

She was in a new version of *Jane Eyre* for the BBC, as well as starring in a new drama about artists in the 1960s called *The Invention of Colour*. She was all over everything from the *TV Times* to the highbrow and middlebrow supplements. She posed in glamorous dresses for the glossy magazines as well as being interviewed for the *Guardian*, where she was prompted to say she didn't like being objectified. She co-operated fully with all-comers.

By 2006 Gloria was a national and international celebrity, and little Melinda, at three, could see her mother on television and in the papers, when she was not available for a personal appearance. Of her father she saw a great deal, although even he was busy during the day answering the phone to people who wanted to speak to his wife. He must have been delighted to hear the voice of someone he knew.

'Troy, mate, how's things?'

'Well, I have plenty of them, if that's what you mean.'

'Daddy, who is it?'

'It's Uncle Troy.'

'Why?'

'He'll speak to you in a minute.'

Troy wasn't sure if he should ask Leonard if he was working. Without a doubt, he would say if he was.

'Are you still a domestic cyborg?'

'Yes, but it's the last series. After that...I don't know. Do they still do *Crackerjack*?'

'No, gone the way of all flesh.'

'Then I'll be back in the dole queue by the look of things.'

Leonard didn't take the bait about his own career, so Troy assumed that it was non-existent. One thing that was certain about Leonard was that if he had something to tell, he would tell it.

'How's Gloria?'

'You know as well as I do if you're attentive to the news. Anyone who works for the press sees more of her than I do.'

There was a definite note of bitterness in Leonard's voice. He sounded as if he had accepted that he would never work again.

'Listen, Leonard, it's 2006 now.'

'Yes...so?'

'It'll soon be time for the second meal.'

'Meal? What meal?'

Troy reminded him.

'No, mate: that was in case we drifted apart, wasn't it? Anyway, Shirley is...'

'No, the agreement was regardless.'

Troy could hear Melinda explode with joy as her mummy arrived home.

'I'm not sure I'll have time,' she said when Troy managed to speak to her. 'There's a lot going on.'

Gloria also mentioned Shirley's loss in an oblique manner, but Troy replied,

'To tell you the truth, I think it's more of an obligation now that she's gone: it's kind of a remembrance.'

Gloria promised she would make time for it. Troy was disappointed when she had to ask when. Then he spoke to Melinda, who told him what she was doing with some Lego.

By a miraculous lapse in the savage laws of economics, the restaurant in Islington at which they had their original meal was still in business. Gloria and Leonard were late, but Troy knew that they had a busy schedule, so he was indulgent. And he was pleased to see them when they eventually arrived. Once they were all seated, Gloria said, 'This feels so strange. I mean we know each other, but we have a reunion meal.'

'It was agreed,' said Leonard, sounding like a member of a secret cabal. They ordered wine and drank a solemn toast to the absent member of the quartet. At first, they shared a strange feeling of awkwardness. For the first time in five years, they found conversation difficult. But after a few stilted career questions and responses, and Troy's query about who was looking after Melinda, Gloria suddenly became animated.

'I've been reading this amazing book...'

'Oh, not the book!' said Leonard.

'It's a wonderful book and everyone should read it.'

'What's it about?' asked Troy politely.

'Everything. I mean literally everything.'

'Oh, yeah? Big book, is it?'

'Oh, listen...it's literally about everything: life, death, the meaning of life...It's by this Malaysian guy who's like a Swami...or something.' Leonard interrupted.
'There's a new independent theatre opening in Hackney.'
'Great.'
'He helps people come to terms with suffering and...you know, bereavement...'
Troy smiled to acknowledge both conversations. He wondered what sufferings Gloria had encountered recently. Yes, there was Shirley, but he had been the worst affected and he had no need of a swami.
'Anyway, they're funded by the Arts Council or something. They mainly deal with improv.'
'Comedy improvisation?'
'No, no; serious stuff. They're going to be having a sort of open audition soon and...'
'Anyway, I think you should read this book, Troy. You really will...'
She was interrupted by a diner asking for her autograph. She complied with grace and charm, thanking the man for his request, even though his approach had been brash and full of entitlement. Why anyone would pay tribute to a celebrity by asking for a trophy, while at the same time demanding a familiar equality, will never be known. But it happens a lot. They were interrupted again by the arrival of the food and then recommenced their frenzy of interjections and counter-assertions.
'He's coming to London and Leonard and I are going to hear him speak.'
'It's going to be political improv. Should be good. One of the directors is a friend of mine...'

'He really sorted out a friend of mine who is having a lot of anxiety at the moment.'

'...Well, I say 'director' but it isn't really that sort of boss-man role...we'll all make contributions. I'm really excited about it.'

Gloria's presence meant that a lot of the other customers were watching them. They may have thought from the frenetic pace of the conversation that they were drinking a lot, but they weren't: they hardly had time. When Troy could get a word in edgewise, he asked Leonard to elaborate on the political side. None of them had ever been 'spiritual' or religious or political before. This was a new departure.

'Well, you know...issues and that. Modern issues. Contemporary stuff...'

'I think Swami Kandar will be the one to sort out the issues of the world,' said Gloria, in her first direct response to her husband.

After that, they settled down and began to relax. Leonard's discovery of a hopeless dramatic cause allowed Troy to suggest drinking to both their successes. Suddenly, Gloria remembered the real news of the night.

'We've seen a beautiful new house. It's out in the wilds. Do you want to see it?'

'Tonight?'

'Why not? There probably won't be a better time.'

'Erm...OK. Why not indeed?'

They finished eating and complimented themselves on keeping the tradition. It was agreed that they would do it again in 2011, whatever their situation.

'That's a date then,' said Troy.

They both waited while Gloria went to the bathroom. This gave Leonard an opportunity to ask something which had been concerning him for a while. More important than improv, or Gloria's career or his lack of one, or Swami Kandar and the problems of the world or the loss of Shirley or anything.

'Troy, mate, something's bothering me. Do you think I'm going bald?'

Troy hadn't noticed, but now he looked at his friend's hairline.

'I don't think I would describe it as going bald, mate. You've got some little indents at the side where your temples start, but everyone gets those. It's nothing. A lot of men start to recede slightly in their thirties.'

'I'm not thirty yet. Anyway, *you* haven't.'

'Irish mother, mate.'

Leonard wasn't sure if he liked that. He seemed to wonder why he hadn't some Irish ancestry. But Troy could see his concern, so he sought to reassure him.

'No, you're nowhere near going bald, Leonard.'

'It's the last thing I need.'

Troy nodded understandingly. He had read somewhere that nine out of ten men don't really care about going bald, but the other tenth really, really care. That one tenth would almost certainly include Leonard. Gloria returned and they made their way to the car.

A teenager might have thought of this late-night trek into the country as an exciting adventure. Troy was tired and they would be going in the opposite direction to where he lived. But he considered that their meal together was a special moment and that it would have been churlish to refuse. And of course, he was curious to see the house. They sped on into the night with Gloria at the wheel. It didn't take too much time to drive across London and they were soon on the M23 towards Brighton. It was a clear, beautiful night and the weather hadn't started to get really cold yet. Troy asked them about the house, but they wouldn't tell him anything.

'It's a surprise,' they kept saying.

Troy didn't know where they were exactly, being more familiar with the Midlands. But they were clearly in a very affluent area.

'This is it,' said Gloria.

It was dark, but the house was lit up and looked very impressive. It looked like it might have about ten bedrooms and was set in quite a few acres of ground. Troy couldn't believe that he knew people who could afford to buy such a place.

'What do you think?'

'Isn't it lovely?'

'Breath-taking. Melinda will love growing up here. I warn you, though, she'll nag you for a pony.'

'She can have one if she wants,' said Leonard.

'She certainly can. We'd take you in but it's late and the present occupants might think it was a bit weird to go visiting at this time of night.'

'We just wanted you to see it. You can come and stay here for weekends.'

'I could move in. You'd never know I was there.'

'Any time you want to stay, you'll be welcome. Bring a friend,' said Gloria.

'A friend? I could bring my whole family. We'd never leave.'

Gloria parked the car in a layby. The road was deserted and quiet. They stared at the magnificent mansion. Suddenly, a light appeared in the sky and started moving west, following an erratic path. It was too fast to be a private plane.

'What's that?' asked Gloria.

'Some kind of military jet,' said Troy, who had been an aeroplane aficionado as a young boy. There wasn't anything he didn't know about fighters, fighter bombers, airliners, cruising speeds, take-off speeds, bomb loads and trajectories. He could tell by the shape and acceleration that it was probably a military fighter.

'No, it was weird. Moving very oddly,' said Gloria.

'Very odd,' added Leonard.

Troy didn't like the way this conversation was moving.

'Trust me: it's a jet,' he said firmly.

'No, it can't be. It's a UFO,' she said. There was a tone of wonder in her voice.

'I really don't think so.'

'It might be,' said Leonard. 'Doesn't move like anything I've ever seen.'

'We've seen a UFO!'

'We've seen a jet plane,' said Troy. 'It was just moving at an odd angle.'

They got back into the car. Leonard took the wheel.

'Leonard, it was a UFO, wasn't it?' asked Gloria.

'I'm not sure. It might well have been. It was very strange.'

'I can't believe it,' she continued, her conviction strengthening. 'We've actually seen one.'

'I do know someone who saw one once,' said Leonard as he started up the engine. 'He was a really level-headed bloke. Not the sort to fantasise.'

'I'm a really level-headed bloke too,' said Troy. 'It was a jet plane.'

'When was that, darling?'

'Oh, before I knew you. Someone at RADA.'

'Well, I know loads of people who've seen one.'

'I should imagine it's very common. They can't all be wrong.'

Troy left them to it. It seemed to be bringing them together.

'Yes, they're always intelligent people. It's a myth that they're always stupid.'

'It's like the mystery of Elvis Presley.'

'Mystery of Elvis Presley? What mystery?' asked Troy. But no-one replied.

And so they went on, convincing themselves, one hand washing the other. Leonard seemingly wanted Gloria to give him permission to believe it. Perhaps in future days, they would look back on it as one of their cherished, loving memories: that night we saw the UFO. Troy felt like a cad for trying to take it away from them. They drove off. The thing in the sky disappeared but became ever more clear in their minds.

They reached north London at about 2.00am and dropped Troy off. He invited them in for coffee and was delighted that they thought it was a bit late. He had regular, well-paid work now, yet he was still living in a place he was ashamed of. It was time to take stock. His two friends were moving into a house where they would have to pay more than Troy's monthly rent to get the lawn cut, while he had a place that was on the watch list of the local health department.

CHAPTER FIFTEEN

It was a few months before Troy saw them again, although emails and phone calls were exchanged. Amazingly, however, it was Gloria who called him. This was a surprise because it was normally Troy who contacted them – and she was especially busy now. After exchanging the usual pleasantries and jokes, she asked him if he would like to come and stay.

'I was hoping you'd ask: I'm looking forward to coming. I want to see the house from the inside. I bet the inside's bigger than the outside.'

'Not this weekend. I've got *Hello* magazine coming to do a photo-shoot and interview...'

'Very glamorous. I'll make an appointment at the dentist so I can read it.'

They arranged the weekend after and there was a pause which Troy sensed was meant to be awkward.

'Erm...I hope you don't mind me telling you this...it's about Leonard.'

Oh, bloody hell! thought Troy. *What's happening? They're not divorcing, surely?*

'OK,' he said.

'He's written a book.'

'Well, that's fantastic, isn't it?'

'Oh, yes of course. He'll probably want you to read it at some time.'

'Well, sure, I'll be happy to. Certainly got plenty of time on my hands. Tell him to email it to me.'

That couldn't have been the reason for the awkward pause, could it?

'Look, Troy, when you read it, please be positive, whatever you think.'

'Well, naturally. I wouldn't be needlessly destructive. Anyway, it'll only be a first draft, won't it? I'll be constructive in my criticism. Who knows, I might not need to make any.'

'It would mean a lot to him if you liked it.'

'Perhaps I will like it. But if I don't, I'll be gentle with him. I promise.'

Troy couldn't work out what was going on here. Leonard had written a book. They wanted him to read it. He would be glad to. What was the big deal?

'Thanks... erm... it's not a first draft. He's actually found a publisher.'

'Well, there we are then - somebody likes it. I know how difficult it is to get a book published.'

'Not if you know a publisher, it isn't.'

Ah, yes, he thought, *and not if you're married to Gloria Greatorex*. So that was it: rushed into production without too many questions asked.

'Well, I'll look out for it at Waterstones.'

'Oh, we'll send you a copy when it comes out.'

'Then I shall look forward to seeing it.'

'Thanks, darling.'

Melinda, like all little children, could sense something was going to happen, even before the team from *Hello* magazine arrived. She responded by running about a lot in her spacious home. There were two staircases, so she could go up one and down another. This was a very special kind of adventure and she had a special set of noises to accompany the activity.

The representatives of the glamorous periodical arrived at 10.30am on the Saturday. The interviewer was an exquisite forty-something called

Mandy. She was accompanied by a photographer called Dave, who was dressed entirely in black and said 'legend' or 'nice' on the rare occasions when he said anything. Gloria was dressed in some amazing red lacy creation. Melinda loved it. There would have been hell to pay if she hadn't had a new dress to wear as well. Leonard came into the lounge and introduced himself. Mandy and Dave shook hands with him but betrayed bewilderment that he was wearing a trilby indoors.

'Where do you want me?' he asked, a question which evoked even more bewilderment since they really wanted him out of the way.

Mandy said, 'I'll get back to you. We'll do Gloria first.'

Dave nodded in agreement and said, 'Nice'.

Dave sat Gloria on the sumptuous white sofa and arranged the flowing dress over it. It was almost spring, and the french-windows were open. The billowing white curtains made an atmospheric fantasy backdrop. Leonard managed to hold Melinda back, since she obviously wanted to rush in to make a contribution. Perhaps she would grow up to be like Shirley. She wasn't too sure what was happening, but she knew it was big medicine.

'Am I OK to ask questions while we take the pictures?' asked Mandy.

'By all means.'

'So, you're off to America soon to make another film?'

'Yes, in about ten days.'

'With the family?'

'Oh, no. At least, not yet. I'm not planning to leave England.'

'What if they make you an offer you can't refuse?'

'I'll refuse it. Family comes first.'

Mandy asked her about the film, which turned out to be a romcom called, *This Isn't It!'*. Was she looking forward to working with Brett Renkler? You bet she was.

Not wanting to be churlish, Mandy asked Leonard a few questions. How did he feel about being a househusband? She meant well and was only trying to include him, but it wasn't the best question.

'I'm not going to be anything of the sort. I'll be working on my second novel.'

'Your second novel? I didn't know you'd written a first one. That sounds very exciting.'

She knew better than to ask him what the first one was about, but he told her anyway. There was no stopping him. He was very excited about it, he said. Mandy could tell he was. Eventually Melinda put her hand over his mouth and said, 'Daddy, stop saying things'.

A Polish woman, whose job was never properly defined or described, as she was clearly a servant, had prepared a buffet lunch. Her name was given as Mrs K, since her real surname was likely something phonetically impenetrable. She was built like a circus strongwoman.

Mandy and the dark photographer got stuck into the food while Gloria went upstairs with Melinda to get changed into a jacket, A-line skirt and boots for the next part of the shoot, which would be outside the stables. Not for the first time, Melinda wanted to know why there weren't any horses in them. The duo stayed until about 3.00pm. They had overshot their allotted time, they said. It often happened, they said. They apologised to Leonard, explaining that they wouldn't be able to take any photos of him.

The week after, Gloria collected Troy from the station in a large car which almost resembled a military utility vehicle. She was delighted to see him. Fame hadn't spoiled her in the least.

'Leonard looking after Melinda?' he asked as he got into the car.

'Yes, he's well trained.'

She smiled brightly but Troy could sense another of those awkward moments. As they drove to the house, he decided to be a bit more assertive.

'Go on; let's have it.'

'What do you mean?'

'You collected me on my own because you wanted to talk to me alone. Is it Leonard?'

'Oh, there's nothing really wrong. I mean, in many ways our life is enviably blissful.'

'So what's the problem? Is he OK?'

'He's fine really. He's just well...getting a little obsessive. That's why I'm glad you're here. I'm hoping you'll pull him out of himself.'

'And here's me thinking you invited me because you liked me.'

'Oh, Troy, don't be so awful. It's because we like you that we want you to be here. You'll be just the tonic for him.'

'So, what's wrong exactly?'

'Nothing I can put into words. He's started reading the *Guardian*.'

'Good; that'll double their circulation, won't it?'

'He doesn't just buy it. He reads it.'

'Bloody hell. Get him checked into a Swiss clinic immediately.'

'Oh, Troy, stop. He reads articles from it out to us over breakfast and he gets very animated.'

'Well, I don't know what to say. He's reading the same paper as everyone else in Equity and the BBC. It's hardly going to be deadly to his acting career - unless he's planning to move into trading oil futures.'

'What acting career? He doesn't have one.'

They arrived at the large gates of the house. She pressed a switch on the car dashboard and the large metal gates opened.

'You'll see what I mean, anyway.'

Leonard, holding Melinda, was waiting to meet them at the huge double front door. It was so large that Troy wondered if Gloria was going to drive the car into the hallway.

Once inside the house, the two men shook hands. Troy thought Leonard looked perfectly normal and genial (although he was wearing a shooting cap indoors). Melinda was a little wary of Troy at first. He found it almost impossible to believe that the progeny of Gloria Greatorex and Leonard Newton could be shy.

It was late so they went straight into dinner. The dining room was the size of an airport departure lounge, if not an actual airport. There was a huge bowl of fruit in the middle of the table. Troy took three apples and showed Melinda how he could juggle. After that she decided she liked him again and followed him around, asking him to do more tricks. Once they had sat down, the giant, mysterious Slavic domestic brought soup which Melinda said she didn't like before she had tasted it. Then Leonard was off.

'Did you see that report in the Guardian today, mate?'

'Er...no. What about?'

'About how much the world spends on arms.'

'No, I think I missed that. Good fun, was it?'

Good fun wasn't the term; clearly, it had excited Leonard a lot.

'Oh, darling, Troy doesn't want to hear about defence spending while he's eating.'

'All right, I'm just saying. You ought to have a look at it. I'll show it to you later.'

'Look forward to that, mate.'

'Don't you read the papers?'

'No need, really. My cleaning lady tells me what's in the Daily Star, so I keep fairly well informed. She knows more about what's wrong with the country than she does about cleaning. Anything she doesn't know I can get from the taxi drivers.'

'You must be bloody joking, mate.'

'I think he was, darling,' said Gloria.

'I want an orange,' said Melinda.

After dinner, which was pleasant, as well as being informative on the subject of the National Health Service, they went and sat in the lounge and had coffee.

'Tell Troy about the book, darling.'

It was the best she could do to get him off comprehensive school funding. Leonard told him about the book. It had been rushed into publication and would be out quite soon.

'They normally move quite slowly in publishing,' said Troy.

'You're not kidding.'

'Well, I'll look forward to it.'

'I can get you a sneak preview.'

'Great.'

And the conversation drifted towards more relaxed topics than national and international governance. Melinda went to bed after demanding that Troy do some juggling again. She was so excited that she wanted to take the apples upstairs with her.

'Anyway,' said Troy after Gloria had returned and sat cosily on the sofa next to her husband, 'never mind us. Tell us about America.'

'I'm off on Monday for a script reading. Back at the weekend, then away again.'

Leonard looked agitated and said something about the contribution of jets to global warming. Troy could see what was worrying Gloria: he was creating a defining role for himself with the only thing that was left: politics.

'Oh, that reminds me,' said Troy. 'What happened to the improv group? You were quite excited about that, weren't you?'

'Oh, yeah. It's still going, but interest sort of fizzled out. People were dead keen at first and then…you know…too much trouble.'

'That's a shame. It sounded promising.'

'Yeah, well… A lot of things do.'

Troy nodded. He noticed also that he hadn't heard anything about Gloria's Swami either. Both of them nine-minute wonders.

He tried again with America and Gloria's bright future, but Leonard got it back on to defence spending. Troy wondered if he had lacked diplomacy raising the subject, because her good fortune was a threat. But they were married, for goodness sake: he had to live with it. And their life together wasn't going to find a solid basis on political statistics. Gloria saved the evening by suggesting Trivial Pursuits. Leonard won, which put him in a much better humour.

CHAPTER SIXTEEN

They took a lot of photos of Gloria at LAX airport when she disembarked. She was very tired from the journey but managed to glow for the reporters. A car the size of an oil tanker took her to the hotel. It was still early so she could go down to the pool for a swim. But, as soon as she got outside, there were more photographers waiting to ambush her. She had never been this famous in Britain. But clearly, the marketing department of the film studio had been hard at work to promote the magnificent creature from England who was going to take Hollywood by storm.

Back in her room, she got a call from someone on behalf of the studio telling her to relax and enjoy herself today. A car would pick her up tomorrow. She rested in her room until it was time to eat. Once downstairs, the cameras and phones started clicking again.

The next day the car came as arranged and Gloria was taken to the rehearsal/reading room. The rooms were very different from the sheds which the BBC used for these kinds of occasions. This was Hollywood: the litter bins would be hand-crafted and flown in specially from Italy.

The director, a woman called Lisa Krenova, was there to greet Gloria with great warmth. After being served coffee by an elderly barista behind a counter, who treated her as if they were both lifelong friends, she sat at the reading table. There were a few actors at the table who gave her friendly greetings but then formed a clique and whispered to each other. Not all of them would be acting in the film but were just there to help out until all the parts had been cast. Most of the action revolved around Gloria and her male co-star, Brett Renkler, an already established star.

The next person to arrive was a small, squat woman of about seventy. She gave only her first name as Antonia, clearly expecting everyone to know who she was. She greeted Gloria as if they were lifelong enemies, but mercifully sat down the other end of the table, as if she were afraid of catching something. Gloria discovered that she had once been a famous character actress in an ancient but long-running US comedy show. Now she mainly just helped with readings and bit parts.

Brett Renkler arrived late, of course. Like Gloria, he was on the way up, although further up the American ladder than she was. Gloria noticed how short he was, but like her own husband, he compensated with a powerful charisma. His facial features off screen seemed craggy and exaggerated in real life. They both smiled and shook hands. They seemed to like each other, which was good, since a lot would depend upon the way they interacted on film.

'Hey Gloria. Great to meet you.'

'Likewise, Brett. Nice to meet you.'

'Wow, that is one hell of an accent.'

'Oh, well, thanks. I can do others if necessary.'

'No, you're good. Don't change a thing,' he replied smiling.

He seemed like the only normal person in the room.

'OK,' said Krenova, 'if we're all good to go, then let's make a start.'

So, they began to read the script.

It was an easy first day. They started at around 10.00am and with various breaks, were done by 4.00pm.

'Great stuff, kids,' said Lisa. 'Same time tomorrow.'
'That went well,' said Renkler to Gloria as they prepared to leave.
'Yes, it did. I've got a good feeling about this film.'
'Well, from what I hear, anything you're in is a hit.'
'I heard the same about you. But as my agent is fond of saying, we're all bankable until we're not.'
'Maybe you'd like to grab a coffee at my hotel. It's nearby.'
'Oh, that's very sweet but I must get back. I've things to do – and lines to learn.'
'We could go over them together.'
'Not just now, thanks.'
She scratched her eyebrow so he could see her wedding ring. Then she smiled, said goodbye and left. The car took her to the hotel. She knew he would ask her again.
Back in her room, she called Leonard and Melinda.
'How did it go?'
'Good. I think it will be a good film.'
'What film?'
'I told you, mummy's in a film, like on television.'
The next day, the car came and took her to the same place. This time they built on the previous day's work, going over the script and developing ideas and intonations. Everything went well and Krenova said that they would be looking to start tentatively rehearsing a few scenes.
Again, at the end of the day, Renkler asked her to have coffee with him and she again declined. Once again, she said that she wanted to learn

her lines and he said that it would make sense for them to do it together. Gloria thought he was attractive – naturally, since that was what he was paid to be - but he wasn't irresistible. There is no such thing as somebody who is irresistible.

By the end of the week, the characters and motivations were starting to take shape. Suggestions had been made and writing changes requested, but nothing major. There were no prima donna arguments which affected the schedule or the atmosphere of the nascent project. It was all going horribly well.

Once again, Renkler had repeated the offer of a coffee at his hotel and this time she had said yes. Once at his hotel, he suggested that, as it was Friday, they could chance a drink. When she told him she didn't really drink, his aspect seemed to change, as if she had thrown a wrench in his plans; as if not drinking represented some kind of pious judgment upon people who do.

'I'm only suggesting a drink,' he said sharply. 'I wasn't planning to go to an opium den and get wasted.'

Then he suggested that they go upstairs to his room. When she declined, he suddenly changed. In full view of the hotel customers in the lounge, he started yelling at her.

'Who the f*** do you think you are? Another crummy limey nobody sticking your nose into the trough of American plenty. I'll bet you're a g*******d socialist as well.'

Gloria was horrified and speechless.

'Brett, control yourself,' she hissed. 'Do you want this to get into the papers?'

He lowered his voice but was just as nasty.

'You think you're gonna get to the top with your legs closed, you prissy bitch? You're dreaming. F*** you.'

And with that he stormed out.

Gloria hadn't been frightened because there were people watching. But no-one had made the slightest attempt to intervene. Not even the staff. She got a taxi back to her hotel. Once in her room, she began to cry. She had to make a film with this man. What was she going to do? Go back to England? Well, she was going back anyway. She could make that decision later. Then she remembered that Leonard would be with her on the next trip. His presence would counteract any temptations or trials which arose. Brett's behaviour had been disgusting and inexcusable, but perhaps she shouldn't have accepted his invitation. She wouldn't again.

CHAPTER SEVENTEEN

Monday morning brought the moment that Troy had been dreading. He got out of bed and answered the door to the postman. He had a parcel; it was from Leonard. He recognised the giant extrovert handwriting with the circles above the 'i's. It was a copy of his new novel, which had recently been published. The small note inside simply said,
Well, Troy, me boy! Here it is! Enjoy! Regards, Leonard. PS Let me know what you think! Don't be shy! (I know you won't be.)
Underneath, he had drawn a little cartoon of a thumbs-up with a smiley face. Well, Troy was glad that Leonard was in such good spirits. If this book were good then, even if it didn't sell well, it could be just the medicine for Leonard to get his self-esteem back. He couldn't wait to read it.
These days, it is the devil's own job to get a novel published, even though – and probably because – the arrival of IT makes the writing of it easier. It wasn't until Troy started to read it that he realised just how remarkable a feat getting it published had been. The book was called *Klab*. It was about a man called Robert Klab. Klab was a very great actor, wit, musician, writer and general Renaissance man who was misunderstood by the philistines of the world. Only he knew of his own greatness. So said the blurb on the back. Klab was of short stature but had a very great charisma. Women found him very attractive.
Troy took the book back to bed with him and began to read. The story began with a piece of introspection in which Klab took stock of his life. It continued that way for fifty of the novel's three hundred pages.

Nobody could accuse *Klab* of lacking character development. It was just that it contained little else – and only one character was developed. In accordance with the traditions of writing, the first novel was strongly autobiographical. Troy had never realised that Leonard's life had been so uneventful.

Klab wandered past the old cinema in the rain. It was closed now. He had once gone there with his school friends to see all his favourite films. It was raining hard. The rain ran off the cinema roof and cascaded onto the pavement. He thought of rainy days when, as a child, he had attended this cinema or others. None of his friends could have guessed that he, Klab, would surpass all those stars of the silver screen in talent and charisma…

Troy looked at the clock on the bedside table. He felt strangely drowsy. But out of loyalty to his friend, he ploughed on.

Once the cinema – that drab, Greystone building - had been alive with his childhood dreams. Now he felt that his life had been washed away by the rain. He wandered on and came to the old school. Another drab building full of drowning memories. Klab had been very popular at school because of his wit, charm and athletic prowess - and yet he had also been strangely alone, isolated by his own genius. He took a deep breath and closed his eyes in despair. Time seemed to stand still. He felt exhausted and lacking in hope…

Troy took a deep breath and closed his eyes in despair. Time seemed to stand still. He felt exhausted and lacking in hope. He was really bonding with the character. He decided that he needed some coffee. Maybe with some brandy in it. After going downstairs to make it, he returned and took up the struggle once again.

He read diligently on for a while. He felt pleased by his efforts: it was a good exercise in character building. He felt like an old pioneer striding towards the North Pole with the wind against him. He continued reading, his fingers pressed tensely against the sides of the book. Then he looked at the time. Only an hour had passed. It had seemed like so much more. He was relieved that so little of his life had been wasted in the task of assessing *Klab*. He put the book to one side. Reviewers never read the entire book. Why should he? He was a busy man. He lay back on the pillows and drifted into a merciful sleep.

CHAPTER EIGHTEEN

Filming of *This Isn't It!* finally got moving. This time Leonard and Melinda were to come over with her. Melinda was a little upset by the challenge of sitting still for about twelve hours. But the trip was uneventful for her: she slept through a lot of the turbulence which turned some of the adult passengers white. Mrs K, who had been brought over to help look after the child, looked as though she was about to bail out. They arrived in Los Angeles early in the morning and were taken to a luxurious chalet in Beverley Hills. They had the whole day to themselves. Shooting would begin the next day.

There was a party that night at the director's house, also in Beverley Hills. The house was big enough to contain Gloria's three times over and had a reception area lavish enough to rival a major port. The party itself was a relaxed and informal affair with only one band playing at the bottom of the rolling plains of the garden (presumably so they couldn't be heard at the top). Leonard was the only guest wearing a hat.

Lisa Krenova introduced them to various people: some celebrities, some hangers-on.

'There's a lot of lawyers here tonight,' she said to the couple, winking, 'so be careful what you say.'

'The first thing we do, let's kill all the lawyers,' said Leonard in his booming theatre voice. Some of the guests looked round in surprise. Not many of them recognised it as a quote from Shakespeare, and in any case, there is no limit to what people can take offence at these days, especially lawyers. The couple drifted round and tried to mingle. They might have expected it to be easier to talk to people in America, rather than in reticent England, but this place seemed very cliquey. Krenova introduced them to a very prepossessing middle-aged man.

'This is Sam Felden. He's one of the biggest agents in the country.'

The man smiled at Gloria.

'Great pleasure to meet you,' he said, shaking her hand. After a pause, he shook Leonard's too. The pause was just enough to upset Leonard.

'Nice hat,' he said to Leonard.

'Thanks. Who are you?'

'Who am I? Like Lisa said, I'm one of the biggest agents in the country.'

'My wife already has an agent.'

'What the hell is wrong with you? I just said hello to her,' said Felden.

'I'm her husband.'

Felden's aggressive instincts came to the fore now. He was one of those men who could be friendly and charming when the situation required it, but could snap like a Doberman when riled. You needed both qualities to succeed in business.

'Oh, yes. I know you. You used to be an actor, didn't you?'

'I bet *you* did as well. Most agents fail at something beforehand.'

'Leonard!' hissed Gloria. She took his arm and steered him away after apologising to Felden.

'What the hell is the matter with you?'

'I didn't like the way he spoke to you.'

'What do you mean, 'spoke to me'? He was perfectly polite.'

'Well, I didn't like him.'

'He might have been useful to know.'

'You're on the way up: you don't need anyone now. It's only when you're coming down you need people,' said Leonard darkly.

'Darling, please! This is very important to me. What's wrong with you?'

'Well...' he said uncertainly. Then suddenly, he waved a hand at the sumptuous buffet and said, 'Look at all this self-indulgence.'

Gloria was mystified.

'Self-indulgence? Since when has that bothered you? Good grief, don't you think someone from Africa would think our life at home is self-indulgent? Who are you to judge other people with your advantages? What's got into you tonight?'

Leonard wanted to have the last word, but Krenova came over to take her to meet someone else. Gloria left him and went with Krenova. Leonard wandered about and tried to make friends with little success – although people did stare at his hat. Gloria returned to him as soon as she could. They left early as she had to be up at five. They didn't say much in the car going back to the hotel. She was nervous enough at the prospect of meeting Brett again.

The car came early and took her to the studio, where she went straight to make-up and costume. When she arrived on the set, Brett was there. He was all smiles and charisma and pumped her hand.

'Gloria, great to see you again! Good trip over?'

She was taken aback but managed to respond correctly, which is to say she smiled tightly and said, 'Yes, everything was fine. Nice to see you again, Brett.'

'Let's go get 'em,' he said.

They sat in chairs with their names on the back. Gloria moved hers away from his and studied her script. Brett didn't bother her. He had the attention of a pretty young assistant to keep him occupied. For the rest, the day's shooting went smoothly.

Back at the hotel, she felt greatly relieved that the day's action had gone well. But there was still Leonard to deal with.

'Darling, are you all right?'

Leonard was sitting on the bed, playing idly with Melinda, who was rolling about on the floor giggling.

'I'm OK,' he said sullenly. She sat next to him and put her arms around him.

'Is it...is it all this? Is it hard to take?'

'No,' he said slowly, 'I'm all right, really. I'll be like Frank Sinatra. I'll have my *From Here to Eternity* moment and I'll be back.'

'Not quite like Sinatra, darling. He lost Ava Gardner when he was down. You wouldn't lose me. I'd give it all up to keep you.'

'I haven't lost anything. I'm right in the middle of it,' he said.

She kissed him and put her head on his shoulder.

'We'll be back home soon. You'll feel better then. And there's your book too.'

'Yes, there's the book too,' he said.

Melinda giggled.

'There's the book,' she said.

CHAPTER NINETEEN

Troy was such a busy man that the week passed very quickly. Soon the weekend supplements arrived with the book reviews. They were much more fun than the books. He read the Times first.

Klab is a first novel by the actor Leonard Newton. I sincerely hope that it is not autobiographical, since I might suspect that Newton is in the early stages of catatonia. (As might the reader soon be if he persevered beyond chapter one.)
Then the Guardian.

Klab by Leonard Newton, is a novel about a superhumanly gifted actor, musician, polymath and Renaissance man – and for aught I know, since I wasn't really paying much attention, acrobat, brain surgeon and mind reader. He is called Robert Klab. Poor Klab is apparently misunderstood. Whether he is really misunderstood by the other (rather vaguely drawn) people in the book, or whether they just make a run for it when he makes an appearance, is a moot point which can only be assessed by reading through to the end. I am forced to deduce, therefore, that the answer will never be known. As to the more important question: namely, how the hell did this book ever get accepted by a reputable house? I can only assume that it must be the first novel ever to be rejected by the vanity publishing industry – although God knows there is enough vanity in it.

The Telegraph, however, was the best, describing Klab as *'an endlessly lethal constricting serpent of a monologue, lying in a foetid ditch, bloated by the author's all-consuming passion for the sound of his own voice.'*

Troy was a little depressed on reading these reviews. Klab was not very good, but there were worse novels winning literary awards these days. He felt bad for Leonard but also felt that he had problems himself. He told himself to get a grip. He was still haunted by Shirley's memory and he knew that the ghost would only go when he had someone to replace her. He didn't feel that this was in any way treacherous, since she had betrayed him, and they had parted before she died.

Meanwhile, externally, he had little to complain about. The work was steady, if not glamorous. *Herbert's Hotel* would not be recommissioned but might be repeated, earning him the appropriate repeat fees. He had also appeared in a TV advert and the amount of money paid to him for such a small amount of work had amazed him.

And that reminded him: so far in his career, he had handed his accounts over to his mother to put together. But she was getting old and was pressing him to get a proper accountant who would be more than just a bookkeeper. Tax law is an ever-shifting river of slime that needs expert handling. Having located a firm on the internet, he went over to their tiny office just off the Bakers' Arms in East 17.

He sat in a small, tatty waiting room for a few minutes before an attractive, light brown-haired woman of about his age came out to see him. She was dressed in a plain jumper and skirt and identified herself as Gudrun Guggenbichler.

'Troy Colson.'

She gave him a card.

'Thanks. I'll practise the name tonight.'

She smiled. She had a ready smile for a tax specialist. President Nixon had specialised in tax law. She smiled like him.

'Please come into the consulting room.'

He followed her in, doubting as he did so that they would both be able to fit. After they had sat down, she asked him what he did for a living, preparing to type the details into her computer.

'I'm an actor. If you use *Vortex* razor blades, you'll have seen me on telly.'

'Vortex? Doesn't that mean 'whirlpool'?'

'Yes, but don't try and work it out. People in marketing and advertising are deranged in this country. It's all that cocaine.'

She nodded, as if she had always suspected this but had never dared say so. She typed in a few lines.

'Troy...Colson...date of birth?'

'April 13, 1980.'

'Oh, that makes you a...'

'Please don't tell me what my star sign is. I am not interested in that stuff.'

'Sorry. Address?'

He gave it to her.

'Oh, you live near me.'

'Really? I'm from Nottingham originally.'

She didn't know where this was.

'What about you?'

'I'm German. From Heidelberg.'

'Oh,' he said, 'Heidelberg, eh?'

He so desperately wanted to impress her by naming someone famous from Heidelberg. Or by knowing that the region was famous for its fruity wines, karate schools, flower arranging competitions, weight-lifting midgets, hand-crafted leg-irons and university patisserie department. But he knew nothing about Heidelberg.

'Good place, is it?'

'Heidelberg? Yes, it's a very famous place. Hegel went to the university.'

'Getaway. Well, well. So old Hegel was a Heidelberg boy, was he? Good grief. They kept that quiet.'

'No, no; it is a well-known fact.'

'To tell you the truth, I haven't seen a paper for a few weeks. Anyway, what brings you to London?'

Her reply was precisely what he expected. Her husband had brought her to London. But Troy had already looked and had seen no wedding ring. He made the daring assumption that she was divorced. She confirmed it without his asking. He wanted very much to ask her out but decided that it was a bit too soon. She didn't even know his national insurance number yet.

After she had finished, they stood up and shook hands. Troy promised that he would keep all receipts for everything for the rest of his life, including any bribes in large bundles of used notes from Qatari businessmen. As he walked back to the tube station, he kept looking at her card. It would be very important for him to get the name right. A few days later, as he was trying to think of an excuse to call her, she called him.

'Oh, hello Troy. It's Gudrun Guggenbichler.'

'Hello Gudrun.'

'I just saw you on television. I thought you were joking when you said you were in an advert.'

Clearly, the poor woman was still having trouble negotiating the abstruse vagaries of the British sense of humour.

'How long have you been in this country?'

'Six years.'

It takes longer than that, he thought.

They chatted for a while. In fact, her call was to ask him to stop by again, bringing some documentation and various other bits and pieces. He agreed to bring them in and suggested they have lunch at the same time. She said yes.

They found a wine bar near her offices which served food and, even more miraculously, they found a table. The place was packed.

'I'd better give you these,' he said, handing over a brown envelope.

'Thanks, I hope they don't think we're doing a drug deal.'

'Not in this place: they'll think we're estate agents swapping contracts. Well, you've got my particulars, but I know nothing about you.'

'I don't know anything about *you*. What do your parents do?'

'They divorced a long time ago.'

'Oh, I'm sorry. Why?'

'Well, neither of them could get along with anyone. Perhaps they thought by marrying each other they would cancel each other out. But it didn't work out that way.'

'Well, if they'd married other people, they would have made two others miserable. They spared them that.'

'No, they didn't. They had children. They made us miserable. And the neighbours hated them as well. Everybody did.'

'But you seem very nice and placid.'

'Yes, there's no genetic explanation for that. They were so ashamed of my equable disposition that they hid me away under the stairs for years.'

She paused, lifting an eyebrow to this, then said,

'And you have a brother?'

'Oh, yes. They were very proud of him. He's in jail.'

'Really?'

'No, not really, but he ought to be. I don't know where he is or what he's up to. No good, I should imagine. Last time I heard of him, he was playing bass in a band called *Botched Operation*. There, that's my life story. What about you? I know nothing about you, apart from the fact that you went to school with Hegel.'

'I'm 29. Hegel was born in the eighteenth century.'

'Oh, you just missed him. Shame.'

'He's dead.'

'Well, you can't be a superstar forever. I hope he left enough for the funeral.'

She told Troy about her marriage which had lasted two years before her husband had run off with their Serbian cleaning lady.

'What has he got against English girls?'

'I think he had something against everyone, but I don't want to talk about it. I did history at university.'

'At Heidelberg.'

'Yes, that's right.'

'Hegel went there, you know.'

'Erm...yes. That was before taking an accountancy course in London. Then I did an extra module in British tax law.'

'Well, let's hope you're a good accountant. I'm from Nottingham, like Robin Hood. I believe in robbing the rich – and the richest people I know are the Government. I want to take them for every penny I can.'

'Well, as long as it's legal, we'll try to let you keep as much of your money as we can.'

'I'll drink to that.'

So they drank to it and then arranged a proper date a couple of days later.

CHAPTER TWENTY

'Mr Newton?'

'Yes, that's me.'

'Mr King will see you now.'

Leonard was sitting in the plush offices of the West End Hair Clinic. He was wearing a homburg. His collection of hats was growing to an impressive range. There were two other men sitting there, also wearing hats. This was a welcome and comforting sight; he was among friends. He stood up and followed the hygienic receptionist into the office suite, where he was met by the senior trichologist Gerald King. King was a handsome man whose deeply tanned skin suggested that he had spent more time in the sun than Lawrence of Arabia.

'Hello there. Mr Newton, is it?'

'Leonard Newton, the actor.'

'Well, I'm Gerald King the trichologist. Please take a seat.'

They sat down.

'Right, perhaps we can take the old lid off and have a look.'

Leonard removed his hat. King then asked him to push his hair back. Leonard had recently changed his hair style so that it involved combing his hair forward. King said, 'Hmmm' and then started taking some details. Any diseases or disabilities? Any dietary problems? Any trauma in the last three months? All enquiries regarding morbidity elicited a negative response.

'It's just normal male pattern baldness: androgenetic alopecia,' said the trichologist eventually.

'Is there anything you can do?'

'Well, yes and no. There are things that can retard the hair loss - and in some circumstances bring it back. But it's all a bit hit and miss; there's no guarantee. You'll need to take *Finasteride* tablets and probably also use *Minoxidil* topical application. But you must understand that once you start using them you need to continue for the rest of your life – or as long as you think it's important. The moment you stop, it will quickly revert to where it would have been.'

Leonard seemed agitated and interrupted him.

'But why isn't there any guarantee!? You people have been spending billions on research and we're always being told it's just around the corner, but it never comes.'

'No, that's true,' said King smoothly. 'I'm afraid it's just a fact of life. You may just have to live with it. Of course, if you hold it off for ten years and there is a cure…'

'I don't want to live with it: I hate it.'

Mr King, having nothing else to offer, turned philosopher.

'I'm afraid there are some things in life we just have to get used to because they are unavoidable.'

'All right,' said Leonard sulkily, 'I'll try the course of treatments. We'll see how we get on with it.'

'Excellent. You can buy Minoxidil in Boots. It's called *Regaine*. And your doctor can prescribe *Propecia*, which is the commercial name for Finasteride.'

Leonard nodded forlornly.

'I'll write them down for you.'

'No, it's all right. I'll remember them. I'm sorry if I was rude.'

Mr King spread his hands.

'Some men find it very traumatic.'

But he didn't say what sort of men.

Once he had paid and left the clinic, Leonard was about to turn into Marble Arch, when he had a curious feeling of being watched.

This is it, he thought. *This is how it starts. I've started to think people are following me.*

But he was right. A bearded man across the street was holding a camera and it was pointed towards Leonard. He took a few pictures of him. This man was clearly some kind of professional. The camera looked very expensive, but the man looked like an infested hermit. Either he was a narcotics addict who had stolen a camera to pawn it for drugs or he was a professional paparazzo.

But why would he be taking a photo of him? For all his vanity, Leonard hardly thought a professional photographer would make his fortune by selling a picture of him walking down a street. The next day at breakfast, he found out. Gloria was reading the Daily Mail.

'Oh, my goodness, Leonard! There's a picture of you in the paper!'

He took the paper away from her with unnecessary force. When he saw the article, he nearly shouted with horror. There was a photo of him all right. And there was a caption too.

Husband of Gloria Greatorex seeing West End shrink!

'The bastards! The lying bastards! It wasn't a psychologist!'

Of course, the papers weren't deliberately lying. He knew what had happened: he had been a victim of incompetence and ignorance. Whoever had written the caption had obviously misheard 'Trichology

Clinic' as 'Psychology Clinic', which made for a much better news item. Leonard was burning with anger; there were tears in his eyes. Melinda did not understand what was happening but could see her daddy was upset so she started crying too.

'Everything's going wrong,' he said, as he stormed out of the room.

Gloria wanted to comfort him but had to stay to comfort her daughter.

'It's all right, darling, it's all right.'

She was upset herself. She had assumed media attention would cause her some problems, but she had not anticipated that her family would be harmed as well.

'Hello Leonard. It's Troy. Are you OK?'

'I'm fine. The media got it wrong.'

'I'd worry if they got something right; then the whole bloody world would end.'

'It ended for me a long time ago.'

'Oh, do me a favour. Don't talk rubbish. You're going through a bad patch. It happens. It'll get better.'

'Patch? It's been years. It had better improve soon.'

'Are you crazy? You've got a beautiful wife, a beautiful daughter, a lovely house and you want for nothing. And to cap it all, you're a published author. Listen mate, if my jobs dried up, I'd be working at McDonalds.'

Troy knew very well that this wasn't the issue, but he didn't say so.

'That may yet happen.'

'Oh, get off this. John Lennon did no work for five years.'

'That was his choice. And it was his money.'

Leonard sighed and then asked,
'Any good news your end?'
'My end is fine. I've met a girl. She's German.'
'Good for you. What about work?'
'I've done an advert on telly. That'll keep me going until *The Big Issue* process my application. I had a voiceover as well. For a cartoon. Not exactly international stardom but it's an enjoyable living. You?'
'Nothing. I went for an audition.'
'And?'
'They said, "Oh, yes, you're Gloria's husband, aren't you?" So I walked out.'
'You did what? Why?'
'I didn't want the job for that reason.'
'Who says you would have done? Who says you would have got it? You should have at least tried.'
'I'm past trying.'
There was a tired pause. Then he said,
'Gloria's been given an award by the way. Her performance in *Jane Eyre* went out on PBS.'
'Fantastic. I hope you're happy for her.'
'Yes, of course. Is it so wrong that I want her to be happy for me?'
'No, of course it isn't wrong, but think of Gloria. She loves you. Don't despair: it'll come. Good grief, every actor since Burbage has been through this. I mean every good one that wasn't typecast in the same role for thirty years.'

Troy could hear Melinda wanting to know who daddy was talking to, so he spoke to her for a while. She told him about plasticene. Plasticene was a subject that excited her. She was making animals. Life was so simple for children. Then he spoke to Leonard again.

'When does she get the award?'

'It's a Golden Globe. We'll be going over next week.'

'Is she supposed to know that she's got it?'

'Not officially, but they usually do.'

'I'll make sure I watch the programme, if they show it over here.'

'Do that. And come over some time. Bring…what's her name?'

'Gudrun.'

'Gudrun? Blimey.'

'I know. Germans are better at naming tanks than girls.'

'Does she know you know Gloria?'

'It's the first thing I tell anyone. People knock on my door for money and I tell them.'

'Let me know if you need any.'

'I'm kidding; I'm fine. I have a good voiceover agent and a German accountant: I fear nothing.'

'Fear is what keeps us going, matey. So they say.'

'If that were true, we'd live forever.'

CHAPTER TWENTY-ONE

Gloria and her family left for the States again soon after. There was so much happening for her. Most of the offers and interest were coming from the US, and they were always coming and going. Sooner or later they might have to relocate. That meant Melinda would end up with an American accent. And they would lose their lovely home in Sussex. Life was moving quickly. It was always the same, especially if you were an actor. Either you were becalmed and stranded or caught up in the white madness of the rapids. But poor Leonard was both. It was a unique experience for which he was not grateful.

Meanwhile Troy was out with Gudrun. They had been together now for a while and things were going well enough for them to start arguing about money. They were dining at a restaurant on the night of the Golden Globe awards. Gudrun had driven and her car had malfunctioned.

'I can't believe it. You're a German financial adviser and you drive a bloody Citroen,' said Troy.

They made it back just in time for Gloria's appearance. They spent most of their time at her place. This was her first visit to Troy's.

'My goodness! Do you live here? What a dump.'

'Yes, we like it.'

They turned on the set only just in time.

'And the award for international television performance for an actress, Gloria Greatorex as Jane Eyre.' Then he added, 'in *Jane Eyre*', just in case anyone thought Jane Eyre was in *Lesbian Vampires from Mars*.

The camera was already on Gloria with suspicious prescience. She looked utterly radiant in her black dress. When she stood up, you could see that there was more jewellery than dress. She walked into the aisle and made her way to the stage. Troy got a very uncomfortable feeling when he noticed that Leonard was following her.

'Where the hell does he think he's going?'

Gudrun looked puzzled too.

'Was he in the programme?'

'No; he's nothing to do with it.'

Troy hoped against hope that Leonard wasn't going to spoil Gloria's big moment; but he knew he hoped vainly. Gloria mounted the stage and accepted the trophy from actor Will Merton. After a slight hesitation, Merton shook hands with Leonard. It was only then that she realised he was there. As long as Leonard kept his mouth shut, it need not be a complete disaster. Gloria spoke first.

'Thank you so much. This is a great honour for me...and er...my husband Leonard. We are very pleased to accept it together.'

A good recovery. But Leonard grabbed the microphone. Troy thought he could hear Merton whisper 'quickly'. Only about eleven seconds were allotted to each acceptance speech.

'I'd just like to make a statement about what's happening in the rain forests where many endangered species are under threat of extinction...'

'Great to know you care, *Mr Greatorex...*'

Mr Greatorex! thought Troy. *That's gonna bloody hurt!*

Merton started to applaud and everyone joined in while a previously invisible attendant came and ushered them off the stage. It could have been a disaster, but past experience had led them to be ready for this kind of thing. They knew how to handle it. They had seen a woman dressed as Pocahontas collect an award for Marlon Brando and heard Vanessa Redgrave bore people about the Israel-Palestine issue. These examples of gesture politics were meant to demonstrate how serious celebrities were, but usually came across as the self-indulgence of people for whom every issue is a mirror in which to preen themselves.

'Darling what on earth were you doing?'

They were back at their rented chalet now. Melinda was in bed. Gloria was in floods of tears. They had been silent in the chauffeured limousine on the way back but now she could no longer control her emotions.

'This was my big moment. Why did you do that?'

'I'm sorry, darling. Couldn't it have been *our* big moment? I had to get that off my chest.'

'Why did it have to be tonight? I didn't know where to look. My first award, Leonard, and you ruined it!'

'You have to take advantage of these occasions.'

'For what? You've never expressed any interest in animals. You don't belong to any societies or charities. Where did all this suddenly come from?'

'We've got to take an interest in these things.'

'But you don't take an interest! You waited until the cameras were on me and spoiled my big moment.'

'Darling, some things are bigger than your big moment. Don't be so selfish.'

'Selfish!' she hissed. It was as much as she could do not to scream, but she didn't want to wake Melinda in the next room. A less stable woman might have hit him with the award she was carrying.

'*Me selfish!?* How dare you!'

Luckily, it was then that Leonard's phone rang. It was Troy.

'Hello, mate.'

'Never mind, hello mate. What the hell have you been smoking?'

Troy could hear Gloria sobbing in the background.

'Troy,' she shouted, 'he called *me* selfish!'

It was a good job Troy wasn't in the room: he wanted to punch Leonard.

'You want to get a bloody grip, mate. Stop feeling sorry for yourself.'

'I have got a grip, thank you. I've got a grip on what's happening in the world.'

'I'll get a grip on your neck if I see you. Why don't you grow up? If it's that bloody important, why don't you bloody well go down there and do something about it!'

Troy was normally a placid man. Leonard was shocked by the intensity of his anger.

'Maybe I will.'

And somewhere in the Book of Doom, an entry was quietly made.

'Tell Gloria to lend you the bus fare,' said Troy and hung up.

The incident may have caused domestic conniptions, but it was all part of the pious tapestry of American celebrity. It was news but not big news. And there were more important things happening in the world at the time. A financial meltdown which looked like being God's last warning, came close to destroying the entire Western system. The culprit was a thing called a toxic derivative, which rolled up bad debts with good ones, as if mixing up poisons with fruits and baking them into a pie would make the poisons more wholesome and nutritious, while making the fruit more exotic. Lehman's became a household name, which would have been good publicity if they hadn't achieved their fame by going bankrupt. Nobody had ever heard of them before.

Queues, the like of which had never been seen outside the Globe Theatre, started forming at the doors of banks and building societies. Some people's lives were ruined, but not everybody's. Political activists occupied Wall Street for a while and then got fed up and went home, leaving Wall Street intact. They were meant to be the angry voice of the people and were portrayed as such by the media; but they turned out to be the usual suspects. Another crisis, unforeseen and totally predictable, rocked people's sensibilities for a while but quietly reinforced the deadly and widespread belief that nothing ever really bad happens. Gloria, Leonard and Troy all survived.

As for actors, they were just actors, even in a country where celebrities were treated like gods. The Golden Globe incident was small beer and soon forgotten. Only one reporter called Angela had phoned to ask Leonard about the incident. He had made a rambling reply about Burmese Pythons in the Everglades of Florida. These were an invasive species, introduced by irresponsible pet owners who dumped them in the swamps when they became too big to be manageable. The creatures multiplied like madness, eating everything in their paths short of fully grown alligators.

'You're on the side of the snakes?'

'Well, they're just killing them in cold blood.'

'I shouldn't think there's any other way for reptiles to live or die,' said Angela chirpily. Then she asked him whether he had any sympathy for the native animal populations who were being wiped out. (She misused the word 'decimated'.)

'Well, all the more reason to stand up for them.'

Angela then asked him how long he had been involved in animal rights and if he was a vegan. She was amazed at his reply.

'You're not even a vegetarian?'

'Well...sometimes I am.'

But even Angela was bored now.

The story was printed in some obscure celeb magazine. (*Gloria's husband digs killer serpents.*) It didn't create much interest. Except for Leonard.

CHAPTER TWENTY-TWO

In 2008, Barak Obama campaigned to snatch the presidency from the Republicans. He won. He was welcome to it, some thought.

Leonard and Gloria were soon back in Britain where everyone was much less excitable. It was the spring of 2009 when Troy made another visit to the house in Sussex. Troy and Gudrun drove down on a beautiful vernal Friday evening. Gloria was glad to see Troy again. She was hoping that he could bring Leonard back to earth again – and maybe also cheer him up.

On arriving, Troy introduced Gudrun to everyone, and they sat down to dinner. The table had been moved onto the patio for the purpose. It seemed an idyllic beginning.

'It's a beautiful house,' said Gudrun.

'Yes, we love it here,' said Gloria. 'Do you remember the night we drove down to see it, Troy?'

'Yes I do. It was just after the meal.'

Troy was about to explain to Gudrun what 'the meal' was when Gloria said, 'We saw a UFO, didn't we?'

'Yes,' said Leonard, who was now more certain with the passage of time that it had been an extra-terrestrial craft.

'Erm...' said Troy. He decided that this was not the time to be controversial, so he said, 'Well, it was something anyway. I thought it was a jet plane.'

'It was a UFO,' said Leonard, and Gloria nodded. As Troy was delighted to see them both agreeing with each other, he said nothing else. That would have been the end if not for Gudrun who said,
'Don't tell me you thought it was a UFO, Troy?'
'I didn't say anything. I reserve judgment.'
He hoped that this would be enough to neutralise the issue.
'I would have expected more sense from you,' said Gudrun.
There was an awkward pause, but Leonard was happy to jump in.
'Did you see that article in the Independent today?'
'Oh, give it a rest about the bloody Independent, Leonard,' said Gloria. Troy had never heard her speak like that to anyone in any situation. It was completely out of character. But Gudrun, who seemed to have a strange Teutonic immunity to social embarrassment, wasn't done with UFOs yet.
'I don't know how anyone can believe in such rubbish. It's complete nonsense,' said the woman who read her stars every day.
'Leonard, Troy and I saw it,' said Gloria tightly. This put Troy in a difficult situation, since he had clearly seen a jet plane. He didn't want to look foolish to Gudrun by conceding that he had seen something he hadn't. But at the same time, he didn't want to embarrass his friends by siding with his tactless girlfriend. Luckily, Leonard persisted with his own line of conversation.
'It was a very good article. It's about these Burmese Pythons in the Everglades.'
'Oh, yes,' said Troy. 'I heard about this. They're taking over. Eating everything in sight. Destroying the entire eco-system.'

'Yes, well, they still have a right to exist.'

'So do all the other animals, if there's such a thing as a right to exist.'

'Are you going to go down there?' asked Gudrun.

'Yes, I am. Gloria's in the States later this year, aren't you darling? She's been offered another film part, so I'm going to do something useful rather than get in anyone's way.'

Gloria clearly knew nothing of this and was too stunned to reply. She looked blankly at Troy.

'You're going to the Everglades?' asked Troy. 'To do what exactly?'

'It's part of a protest against the state-sponsored snake hunters.'

Gloria was so shocked, she could only ask,

'Well, how are you going to get in their way? The place is enormous.'

'It's more publicity than anything else. Drawing attention to the issue.'

'Well, this is ridiculous,' said Gloria. 'It would serve you right if you got eaten by a crocodile.'

'Alligators,' said Gudrun. 'They're alligators in Florida.'

'Well, whatever they are, it's dangerous and silly.'

'There's nothing to worry about, darling. I'll be with experts and we won't be there for long. We just want to draw attention to ourselves.'

'You said it,' said Troy.

'Experts in what?' asked Gudrun.

'Oh, animals and stuff.'

And so it went. After dinner, they played a tense game of Trivial Pursuits in near silence. Troy was astonished to see Leonard cheating by rejecting cards he couldn't answer and asking for the next question. But when he objected, Leonard said,

'It's only a game, Troy.'

'Well, precisely: it doesn't matter if you lose, does it?'

'Oh, stop it you two,' said Gudrun, an idiotic comment which attributed blame to the innocent party and provided fifty per cent exoneration to the guilty.

They were all relieved when it was time to retire.

CHAPTER TWENTY-THREE

They didn't see each other for a while after the unfortunate evening. Troy wondered if they would ever speak to him again. But Gloria called him in the autumn.

'Troy, it's Gloria.'

'Hi darling. Great to hear from you. How's it going?'

'It should be marvellous, but I don't feel like it's marvellous.'

'I know. Where are you?'

'We're in the States. How's erm…?'

'Gudrun? We're having a bit of a break from each other at the moment. We need to think about whether we're really compatible.'

'I'm glad to hear it. I didn't like her.'

Troy had never heard Gloria say she disliked anyone before.

'We're not exactly finished yet. Just having a rest. Is Melinda OK?'

'Yes, she's fine. She's too young to be worried about her father, but I am.'

'What's happened now?'

'We went to an exclusive restaurant. He blew up at the waiter and someone took a photo of him yelling. It's been on TV here. You might see it in the papers tomorrow. Oh, Troy, I'm so worried. He's normally a lovely man. I've never seen him this way before.'

'How is he with Melinda?'

Troy was worried about her.

'Oh, he's wonderful with her. He dotes on her, and she adores him. But anyone else…'

'He's feeling his failure. He needs work.'

'I've tried helping him, but he won't take any jobs that I've arranged for him. He wants to get it on his own merits – which I completely understand. He's so clever and talented.'

She was crying now. Troy could only listen.

'I want him to succeed but everything he does fails. And everything I do succeeds effortlessly. It's so weird.'

'Please don't feel guilty about your own success, Gloria. You shouldn't.'

'I know, I shouldn't - but I do. Everything in our life should be wonderful - but it isn't. I just don't understand it.'

Troy wanted to help but he felt so powerless that he felt foolish.

'And now he's getting involved in all this political nonsense.'

Gloria seemed to think of that as an extra problem on top of Leonard's failure. She couldn't see that it had emerged as a direct result of it.

'He's not really going down to Florida, is he?'

'Yes; I can't stop him. Can you call him, please?'

'Of course I'll call him.'

'Try to talk him out of it.'

'I'll do everything I can.'

'I feel something awful is about to happen.'

'Now don't say that; that's being silly,' said Troy, who felt it as well.

When Troy had finished talking to Gloria, he called Leonard, but there was no response. He sent her a text saying that he would try later.

Leonard flew to Miami the next day to meet with a group of animal rights 'activists' who were waiting for him at the airport. The leader was a large, bearded, camouflaged thug straight from central casting. He gave his name as Brandon, although this was probably a false name.

Brandon had learned many years ago that if you hated humanity and wanted revenge upon society, then the best thing to do was to disguise your venom with a fashionable and convenient ideology which gullible people mistook for moral concern. He wasted no friendliness on Leonard as he led him to the car containing the other activists.

'Let's get this straight,' he said, poking Leonard in the chest. 'We don't normally make common cause with meat murderers like you. This is a pragmatic alliance. We tolerate you because you can get us publicity.'

The car turned out to be a large truck with bright lights attached to the top. In the back were two young people, a man and a woman. The woman had spiky orange hair. The second man looked like something out of a zombie movie. They were also both wearing camouflage clothes.

'Hello, I'm Leonard,' he said as he climbed in.

'No names, idiot,' said the girl.

'But you mustn't call us comrades either,' added Brandon. 'We don't allow outsiders to do that.'

Once he and Brandon were in, the car drove off into the night on the long journey to the Everglade swamps. They hardly spoke at all, except to give Leonard instructions as to what to do when they arrived.

'We have a video camera,' said Brandon. 'We're going to publish it on the internet. We'll be wearing masks, but you're here to be the public face of the group. You'll make the statements. We'll tell you what to say.'

Eventually they came to a long strip of road which went through the swamp growth. It was dark now and little could be seen. When Brendan switched the lamps on, they lit up the road strip, but little else was visible in the surrounding countryside. Off the road, there was just silent and intimidating black.

'This is where the snake killers come,' said the girl. 'They pull them out of the bushes on the roadside.'

'The snakes come to the road at night because it's warmer. The tarmac absorbs the heat of the day,' said Brandon.

'Do we make the video now?' asked Leonard.

'Don't be stupid,' said the girl. 'We don't know what we're going to do yet. We'll make it at the end of the night.'

The second man spoke for the first time.

'We'll spread out. Find a part of the bushes and stay there. Try not to be seen.'

He sounded like a voice at a séance. Brandon threw Leonard a camouflage jacket. He began to wonder if he was doing the right thing. But it was too late. He picked up his backpack, got out of the truck and went into the bushes.

'What if someone comes?'

'If the snake killers come, you stop them, obviously,' said the second man.

'By any means possible,' said the girl as she pulled out a gun. Leonard was horrified but was glad to get out of the truck. The others drove off and left him in the eerie silence.

He had been under the impression that they were just going to impede the progress of the snake hunters. Clearly, he had fallen in with a pack of extremists and maniacs who were prepared to kill humans in order to defend dangerous predators that were slaughtering the local wildlife in thousands. What the hell had he got himself into?

He unfolded a small seat and secreted himself in the bushes. He felt a complete fool; all the more because he had no way back.

It was hot, oppressively so. He took out a bottle of water and took a swig. Some lights appeared in the distance. A car approached and then rushed past. It seemed preternaturally loud in the deadly wilderness. There was no sound again. There should have been. He should have been able to hear the sound of birds, foxes, raccoons, rabbits and small cats making their night noises. But they were gone, destroyed by the very invading pythons he had come to protect.

He wanted to phone Gloria and tell her how much he loved her. But he was afraid. And he knew that it would be selfish because she was working on a film. He knew that she would drop everything and fly down to take him back. He felt like a small lost child, a naughty child, a runaway who was scared of the dark. It had been a long time, he knew, since he had thought about others. He had bathed in the slop of self-righteous and trendy political showcasing to draw attention to himself and had been sucked into a cesspool of evil. He had been a vain fool - but he knew himself too late.

He drank some more water. He dozed off, but was awoken by another vehicle which whooshed past. Then he dozed again.

Then he awoke again with a stabbing pain in his ankle, just above the top of his tough walking boots. He looked down while fumbling in his pocket for a torch. He saw with indescribable horror the head of the creature he had come to save. It had sunk its razor teeth into his leg.

He was terrified. Pythons are not venomous, but they have dangerously sharp teeth. This one was enormous. Judging by the size of its head and neck it must have been about eighteen to twenty feet long. This was not unheard of but unusually large for the area. He realised in terror that it was big enough to kill him. He screamed and stood up from his little stool. Then he foolishly tried to run. But the hideous reptile – weighing nearly two hundred pounds – kept its grip and he fell. He rolled over in panic and tried to stand up again, whimpering all the time in fear. He was now in the worst possible position. He was half erect and the snake was able to throw its coils around him. It started to crush the breath out of him. He could feel the cracking of his ribs. It was the last thing he felt.

When Leonard did not return after a day, and did not answer his mobile phone, the alarm was raised. A search was made. They found the bloated, snake first. It was only afterwards that they found Leonard.

No trace was ever found of the other three in the group.

CHAPTER TWENTY-FOUR

Gloria had to be strong for Melinda, otherwise she might not have made the funeral. But she did, and it was the worst part. If she could survive that, she could survive anything.

The vermin from the press were there, taking up seats that should have gone to friends or family members. It should have been a private service, but scum respect nothing.

When Gloria arrived and got out of her car, a reporter who had clearly already started early with his drinking, asked her her husband's name. She was too shocked and upset to say, 'Why don't you google it, you moron.'

Gloria was in black; she also wore a veil. It was a little old fashioned an accessory, but probably constituted a pitiable attempt to shut out the world. She was not crying, since her grief was beyond crying. She was still in a state of shock. She may have taken some medication.

They took their seats in the chapel and Troy sat the other side of Melinda. Gloria held tightly on to her daughter's hand for mutual moral support. Melinda seemed more bewildered than anything. Troy wondered what there was that life could ever give her now. There was nothing. How could a small, vulnerable child ever recover from this?

Occasionally Melinda would look at Troy. He didn't know if he should smile at her. He certainly couldn't say, 'It gets better', because he wasn't really sure if it would be true. He could see no reason why it would be. In any case, it would have been meaningless to her.

The service was led by a preacher doing the worst job of his life. Worse even than a child's funeral, since in this case, the child lives and has to be comforted by mere words.

After the service, Troy was faced with the selfish agony of either going back with them or not going back with them. He knew Gloria's parents would be with her, which was something. In the end, he left the decision to her. She saw him standing there and said, 'Please come back with us, Troy.'

'If you want me to, of course.'

And so they returned to that beautiful house that had symbolised so much glamour and promise for the future. In the car, he sat next to Melinda again. She was still holding her mother's hand. But she looked up at him and smiled tearfully.

'Are you coming back to the house, Uncle Troy?'

'Yes, I'll come back for a bit, if you'd like me to,' he said quietly.

He could see Gloria squeeze her hand and Gloria was able to smile at him as well. It wasn't the usual effulgent and dazzling smile that the world knew, but it was a start. He had never seen such courage.

Gloria's mother, Rhoda, had prepared a buffet earlier. When they arrived at the house, people ate and talked in low voices. There was no alcohol, which was a good thing. People can get very unpleasant when they are trying to drink their way into someone else's misery. Troy grabbed a plate of food – just to keep himself occupied more than anything else - and sat on the sofa. Melinda came and sat next to him.

'Mummy says we're going to America,' she said quietly.

'Will you miss the house?'

She thought for a moment and then said sadly, 'No. I want to go. It's all sunny in America.'

'Yes, it will be good for you and mummy.'

He stayed as long as he could. Gloria was looking tired and he wanted to set an example by leaving early. She saw him to the door and they hugged very hard.

'I know this is an awful cliché, but it does get better. It will take a while but it will get...bearable.'

She couldn't speak, so she just shook her head. He left.

Gloria took Melinda to the States later the next month. The house was sold, they bought a place in Los Angeles and began the impossible task of beginning again. However, the lacuna in her career caused by Leonard's death did no harm at all to her upward trajectory. The offers continued to flood in. For anyone else, it should have been a golden time.

CHAPTER TWENTY-FIVE

It was over eighteen months before Gloria and Troy spoke again. She and Melinda were now permanently living in the United States.

'Gloria, it's Troy.'

'Oh hi.'

'I called you a few times.'

'Oh, I'm sorry. I get so many calls I've started ignoring them.'

'Nice problem to have. How is it?'

'How's what?'

'Well, I mean everything. Let's start with Melinda.'

'She's fine.'

Gloria seemed distracted.

'Well, that's good. What's your next project?'

'Well, I'm going to be a TV superhero. It's called *StarGirl*.'

'Yes, I saw something about that in the press.'

Troy had hoped that she was going to say that she had turned it down. She could do a lot better than garbage like that, but the money would probably have been a temptation too much. And if the show was a hit, it would have made her a household word for years. Who was he to advise against it?

'Well, that's great anyway.'

Gloria sounded as if she wanted to get away. Perhaps she was busy. Well, undoubtedly she was, so he said,

'Look, are you still on for the next dinner?'

'Dinner? What dinner?'

'Well, it'll be ten years soon. It's sort of a tradition.'

'Oh, yes, of course. I'd forgotten.'

Troy suspected that she hadn't, but he said,

'Listen, I understand if you're reluctant. I mean, there are two ways of looking at it. You could see it as a remembrance of…Leonard and Shirley. Or it could be a painful reminder. I will understand if you see it as the latter.'

Gloria hesitated. How could she see it as anything other than the latter? They were not mutually exclusive.

'Well, look, it's basically that I'm not planning to come back to the UK in the near future.'

'That's fine. I'll come over. We haven't spoken for a while. And I'd like to see Melinda too. If that's the only reason…But if you'd rather not…'

'No, no. That's fine. When is it?'

'When is it?…Well…September 11th.'

'Oh yes. I'll see what I'm doing on that date and let you know. Great to hear from you, Troy.'

And she was gone, leaving Troy with the unpleasant suspicion that he was a reminder of the past that she didn't want to hear from. Truthfully, he never expected to hear from her – but he did: she emailed him her schedule. Apparently, there was a window. It wasn't exactly on the 11th, but it was near that date, and he accepted that she couldn't really be expected to drop everything.

He booked a flight and a hotel. It was a big expense, and he was a little miffed that she, with all her financial resources, would not come to London. But she had resources because she was famous and busy.

That's the way of it and there is no middle path, at least not while you are young.

Gloria confirmed his email automatically as if she were affirming a meeting with the money people. Then she sent a follow-up asking him if he needed any financial help. He replied that he didn't as he never went anywhere or did anything and that he was long overdue for a holiday. None of this was true. He was glad that she had been thoughtful enough to ask, but was also surprised to discover that he was proud. He didn't tell her that he had got back with Gudrun, but he wondered if she would actually remember who Gudrun was.

When the date came, he flew out to LAX airport and then checked into an LA hotel. They met in a restaurant which Gloria had chosen. She advised him not to 'go British', which is to say, not to dress as if he had just been cleaning out a septic tank. They wouldn't let him in if he wasn't properly dressed. But he didn't need telling: it was, after all, an important occasion, even if only he thought so.

She was late. He sat at the bar while increasingly suspicious restaurant staff peered at him and wondered if he was some kind of nut who stalked the famous.

But she came eventually, and their attitude changed completely. Gloria seemed harassed but greeted him with a warm hug. The staff relaxed; he was OK. He may not have been famous himself, but he knew famous people. What better reference could there be in life? In California, knowing famous people almost made you famous.

'So, how have you been?' she asked first.

'Well, you know. I'm still alive, still healthy and still working. Voiceovers pay the bills. It's mostly what I do these days and my needs are few. What about you?'

She shrugged. Maybe it was because the waiter had brought the menus.

Then she said, 'I keep going. I keep busy. It's the best way. And then there's Melinda. She gives me a reason to live. And she very much keeps me occupied.'

She stared across the restaurant. Behind Troy was some lucky bastard who may have thought she was staring at him. But she wasn't: she was just looking into the distance. She looked very sad, but she didn't cry. She had done all the crying a long time ago. Even the worst despair reaches a point where there are no more tears. Troy wanted to ask how Melinda was coping with the loss of her beloved daddy; but it was too early in the evening to start digging. He wanted to feel his way. After all, this meeting would open up scars. He was relieved and surprised when it was she who proposed the toast to absent friends. But after that, they seemed to be struggling to talk.

'How are your folks?' she asked desperately. It was just to fill in the gap, but it unearthed more unhappy memories.

'Oh, I lost my father. Heart attack. I tried to call you.'

'Oh, I'm so sorry.'

'But then I realised you never knew him. I hardly knew him myself. He left us when we were young.'

'Oh, yes I see,' she said. This was an odd response. Then without taking her gaze from the distance she said, 'I saw a film about that once'.

He was jolted by such a bizarre comment and could say nothing to it. So instead, he said,

'I was hoping to see Melinda while I'm here.'

'Yes, I'm sure we can do that,' she said. She was back now and had that beautiful smile that melted all the cameras. He smiled back. He felt like a salesman who had sold her a Peloton.

As they finished eating, they chatted idly about the industry – now very different for both of them. Troy began to wonder if this was the last dinner they would have: the tradition now seemed unsustainable. Gloria was only half present at this one. It would be difficult to imagine 2016 being better. But at least it was friendly, and he looked forward to seeing Melinda the next day.

Gloria insisted on paying for the meal and then took him back to his hotel in a car that was too big for the purpose it was meant to fulfil. It was driven by an elderly chauffeur called Jim. She seemed to have an easier relationship with him. She called him 'darling' and joked around with him. Of course, she saw him every day. Troy felt like something of an intruder. But he wanted to go the full distance and see Melinda the next day. When they arrived at his hotel, they hugged and kissed. He got out.

'See you tomorrow,' he said.

'Sure.' She smiled.

On the way back, she relaxed completely, laughing and joking with Jim about various things they saw along the way.

When Troy arrived by taxi at Gloria's home the next day, he was stunned. The place was a palace surrounded by a large wall. He buzzed the house from the gate, and was less surprised to be kept waiting some time. After all, this was America: celebrity stalking with guns was a prime-time pursuit in this part of the world. And if the murderers were really lucky, they got caught and starred in their own show called a televised trial. They achieved the fame they had always sought, if not through creation, then by destruction. And then they could negotiate the book deal in prison. Lawyers would be provided. Interviews with psychiatrists would feed their egos - and vice versa.

After ten minutes, during which he had been fingerprinted by satellite, infra-red brain-scanned and had his DNA checked by the FBI supercomputer, the gate opened and the taxi drove up the meandering driveway. The front door, wide enough to drive a bus through, was opened by Mrs K, the Polish child minder.

'Mrs Newton is not here.'

'Oh, I was supposed to meet her here. I am a friend of hers. We've met before.'

'Yes.' Mrs K remembered him, like she remembered the last newspaper she bought before she left Krakow. Clearly, she was in charge of the household at all times: her responsibilities within had grown as Gloria had retreated from them. But she did have pity on Troy as he had come so far.

'Are you expecting Gloria back any time soon? I wouldn't like to miss her.'

She nodded and showed him into the gigantic lounge. The double doors to the patio were open and Troy could see Melinda lying by the pool in the sun. He walked out to greet her.

Melinda was dark like her father but was clearly going to inherit everything she needed from her mother. She was lying face down on a sunbed trying to read a magazine through sunglasses. She looked up at him.

'Hello, Melinda.'

'Uncle Troy!'

'That's me.'

She got up and hugged him.

'I'm catching some rays,' she said.

She hadn't quite got the full American accent yet, but it wasn't far away. Troy motioned at her to stay where she was while he pulled a patio chair over to sit on. Melinda sat down again. Troy noticed with sadness that she would probably look like Shirley when she grew up. He wanted to know how an eight-year-old child coped with the loss of a father, but he couldn't think of any way to ask.

'Mom doesn't like me sunbathing,' she said, taking off her glasses.

'I'm sure she's only thinking of your health, but I won't tell her.'

If I ever get to see her again, he thought.

'Mrs K will though.'

'I'll back you up. I'll get you a doctor's certificate saying you need more vitamin D. How have you been?'

'I'm OK, I guess.'

Even that was a sensitive question.

'How are you?'

'Well, I'm OK. I'm glad to see you but I'll be glad to get back home too.'

'Do you miss the rain?'

'Oh, definitely. Especially the cold sleet. I have a particular fondness for cold sleet.'

She laughed and said,

'I like rain. It never rains here.'

'The seasons are nice. Why don't you come over some time?'

'Oh, mom's always busy. And she wouldn't let me come on my own.'

'No, but I bet you can persuade her to have a holiday back home. Maybe when you're older you'll come by yourself. But you won't remember me then.'

'Yes, I will. I remember everything.'

Mrs K brought some coffee for Troy and orange juice for Melinda.

'Drink your juice,' she said.

'I hate juice.'

'It's good for you.'

'Everything in America has to be good for you.'

'What about the smog?'

Mrs K smiled at Melinda as she folded up her beach towel. Clearly, she doted on the child. It was stern, old-fashioned doting but it was well meant. Perhaps it was better for her than the kind of New World indulgence that she would get from everyone else. Troy thought maybe Mrs K wasn't so bad after all. She went away and left them alone. Troy chatted with her for a while. How was school? Did she like America? But the last was a silly question: she wanted for nothing here. (Except perhaps for the recent past to be rewritten. But even the LA fixers couldn't arrange that.)

Troy drank his coffee. It wasn't exactly what he thirsted for in the heat. He stayed for about half an hour more and then Mrs K came out with some pretextual task for Melinda that just had to be done right now. He called for a cab on his mobile. When it arrived, Melinda came to the door with him. Between them, Gloria and Mrs K would have made sure she had all the manners necessary to get on.

'It was nice to see you, Uncle Troy.'

'Wonderful to see you too. See if you can get your mum to bring you over sometime.'

'I'll try. You didn't ask me what I wanted to be when I grow up. Everyone else does.'

'Tell me.'

'I'm good at math in school. I want to be an accountant.'

Troy was overjoyed.

'I think that's the best thing you could possibly do. Don't ever go into show business.'

'I won't. Nobody ever has any time.'

The cab came and took him to his hotel. He stayed one more night, but he didn't go to see any of the sights. There are no sights in Los Angeles, unless you are particularly fond of roads.

CHAPTER TWENTY-SIX

A few days later, Gloria was on the set of *StarGirl*. She was having her make-up and hair re-touched by a lady called Sunetra.

'I was so sorry for you, Miss Gloria. It was a terrible tragedy.'

'Thank you.'

Gloria was often hard-pressed to find the right thing to say to this kind of comment. It was kindly meant, and she tried so hard in her career not to be standoffish or to play the diva. (She was too grateful for her luck for that.) She wanted to be polite to everyone but sometimes it was difficult to find a diplomatic way to tell people to leave her alone. And Americans were so direct about everything.

'I read it in the magazine and I cry. You are so young and beautiful. Life is so unfair.'

'I find it gives and takes in equal measure,' she replied flatly. 'Do you think my hair is all right?'

'It's beautiful but I will make it extra beautiful.'

Sunetra went off to find the magical application which would transform Gloria's appearance to a new and numinous level of pulchritude. While she was gone, Gloria noticed that one of the cast, called Belle Demetriou, was sitting next to her. Belle played a middle-aged policewoman who knew StarGirl's secret identity and was her confidante and inside help.

'She's nice Sunetra, but she isn't very tactful.'

'Yes, I'm sure she meant well,' said Gloria.

'It must be so difficult for you,' said Belle, making the exact same intrusion she had criticised Sunetra for. Perhaps she thought being a member of the cast made her closer to the star than a mere make-up girl. Perhaps she thought that she was a confidante in real life. Real life and fantasy were very close together in this world. It took a lot of self-discipline and self-knowledge to keep them separate.

'No, I'm fine, really I am.'

I would be fine if only people would stop prying, she thought. Sunetra came back with the cosmetic lotion which she had wanted.

'Oh, Belle!' she trilled. 'How nice to see you. How are you?'

'I'm great thanks, Sunetra.'

They both chatted while Sunetra teased Gloria's hair to superperfection. They were obviously old friends. Gloria was glad of the break. She wanted to be friendly with everyone, but she wanted privacy also. It was probably the only thing you couldn't buy in Los Angeles. She was English and her grief was to be her own. But now she had to share it with the whole world. She had everything she wanted except the unobtainable miracle of getting Leonard back. She would have swapped it all.

When Sunetra had finished whatever she was doing, Gloria rose from the make-up chair. Just as she was going, Belle leaned over and gave her a business card.

'This guy helped me through a real bad patch. You should call him.'

The card said:

Barry Keeler

Lifestyle Analyst

Confidence and Bereavement a speciality.

'Thank you. It's kind of you to think of me, but I think I just need time more than anything else.'

'Keep the card anyway. You never know when you might need it.'

She went back to the set for more shooting. Or rather, to sit about waiting for a gigantic logistics exercise to be organised in order to capture sixty seconds of indifferent dialogue.

Back home, Gloria hugged Melinda. Mother and daughter still needed each other so badly. They hugged as if one of them were in danger of being taken away.

'Did you have a nice day, darling?'

'Yes. Uncle Troy came. He wanted you to be here.'

'Mummy has to work. That's what pays for this lovely house.'

'I know. I swam for a while. I'm good at swimming.'

'That's nice. I want you to be good at things. You will be if you work hard.'

She wanted to spare her daughter show business. Like Troy, she wanted the best for Melinda: anything but the entertainment industry. It was the Devil that offered you everything and wanted nothing except your soul in return.

CHAPTER TWENTY-SEVEN

Gloria was not in the party mood at the best of times. But big stars have to go out and be seen. It was part of the job, and the agents, managers, fixers and TV bosses who ran the world she lived in would have been angry if she hadn't co-operated. So she went. The trick was to keep the appearances as short as possible. As a general rule, she spent more time getting ready than actually socialising. That was part of the job as well. Gloria was a firm believer in preparation.

The hosts were a producer called Spellman and his wife Laura, once an actress. They were both in their fifties. Laura, on being introduced, gave Gloria a strange, whimsical stare as if to say, *I used to look like you*. But it was without malice; and envy, up to a proximate point, can be a compliment.

Gloria drifted round and chatted to people, just to be sociable, just to be seen. Once she had done her duty, made the rounds and been hit upon by various men - some devastatingly handsome, some arrogant dreamers - she decided to leave. She made her excuses to the Spellmans.

'You know how it is: I have a daughter and she needs me a lot.'

Sure, sure. They understood perfectly. It had been great to see her.

Just as she was going through the door, Spellman called her back and introduced her to a friend of his. His name was Barry Keeler.

Keeler was a typical Angeleno. He was tanned, handsome and in good shape. He was clearly no stranger to the fitness centre. His teeth could have lit up a coal mine. He was attractive, without a doubt. Not enough to blow Leonard out of her mind – only a long time could do that, possibly longer than she had – but he was the first serious proposition she had seen in a good long while. And sooner or later, she knew that she was going to have to say yes to someone. And then she remembered. It was the name on the card Belle had given her.

He didn't look anything like what she had imagined a lifestyle counsellor would look like, in the few microseconds of thought she had given to the matter. He did not resemble your average time-wasting, showbiz hanger-on, preying on the weak and foolish. He looked like the CEO of a large, old industrial corporation.

'Gloria Greatorex! Wonderful to meet you. Love your accent, by the way. You look fantastic. I'm a big fan of your work.'

'Thank you. I can't claim any credit for the accent or the looks, but I have worked hard at my job.'

Barry nodded. He looked at her as if she were the only person in the room. It is a talent that charming people have. Of course, most men looked at Gloria like that, so she was hardly hypnotised by it. But she did think he had lovely blue eyes to go with his light-coloured hair. It looked as if it had been bleached by the American sun.

'Somebody mentioned your name to me the other day.'

'Well, a lot of people know me. I help a lot of people in your business. Of course, we all felt for your terrible tragedy. Somehow – don't **ask me** how – I just knew that our paths would cross.'

'Did you really?'

His pale eyes stared at her. She had read somewhere that having blue eyes actually means that you have no pigment in the iris. Or something like that. Gloria had never met such disarming charisma. And she had met hundreds of men who wanted to try it on with her.

'And we'll meet again, I know we will,' Keeler was saying.

She returned his smile and left. Once in the car she rifled her handbag for the card which Belle had given her, even though she knew very well she had binned it. But she could find him if she wanted. Not that she was in the habit of chasing men. And anyway, she didn't need any therapy: she was confident, sensible and independent. At least, that was what the magazines said. She didn't need a shoulder to cry on. So she told herself.

CHAPTER TWENTY-EIGHT

The plane journey from LAX to London is a grim test of nerves even if you fly well, and Troy didn't. He made a mental note never to go to Australia. And especially not Mars – at least not until they got the warp-drive thing sorted out.

He arrived, shattered, at his flat at 3.00am after fourteen murderous hours of travel. Sleep on the actual plane had been impossible because of the noise of all the children screaming and crying. It's always like this, regardless of what those misleading adverts say about reclining seats on Dreamliners.

He was awoken at 7.00am when Gudrun called him.

'You are back?'

'Only in body; in spirit I crashed over the Atlantic and drowned.'

'I thought you would call me.'

'I didn't get back until 3.00am. I thought I'd get some sleep.'

'Are we seeing each other tonight?'

'Yes, but let me sleep on it and then I'll call you.'

'What time?'

'Gordon Bennett, I don't know! This afternoon.'

He slept until twelve and then she called him again.

'Are you better now?'

'Yes; they found me off the coast of Ireland and rescued me.'

There was a pause.

'Yes, I feel a lot better now.'

They arranged to have dinner at a local trattoria. When Troy arrived, she was already there. It is not a German woman's privilege to be late. She arrived promptly and got straight down to business.

'I looked at your accounts while you were away.'

'Thanks. I hope the experience wasn't too traumatic.'

'Traumatic? I'll say it was. I've never seen such a mess. I had to wade through tons of receipts and stuff. You can't just throw things in a box and expect other people to make sense of it. You need to have a system.'

'I do have a system. I throw everything in a box and expect other people to make sense of it. I'm sending some of my accounts to the Tate Gallery. They're going to put them on display. There's talk of an Arts Council grant.'

'You'll need a grant, the money you are wasting paying tax you don't need to. You need to get yourself organised.'

'Well, there we are: that's where you come in. Anyway, everyone pays too much tax.'

'That's all you know. People who look after their affairs properly pay far less than others.'

'Well, I don't mind paying my whack. I'm not against all tax – within reason. I'm not a socialist but I'm not an anarchist either.'

'There's tax evasion and tax avoidance. They're two different things. Why don't you get a car? You can claim it as work expenses.'

'I can claim all the train tickets, can't I?'

They stopped talking while the waiter, who listened as if he were an undercover agent for the Inland Revenue, brought their food. Then she started again.

'You've got a lot of cash in the bank. You really ought to get a better return on it.'

'Are you my girlfriend or are you trying to sell me a pension fund?'

'I'm both, so you should double take my advice.'

'All right, I will. But not while I'm jetlagged. I might make the wrong decision.'

'All right. We'll talk about it later. How was Los Angeles?'

So Troy told her. He hadn't really seen much of it. It hadn't been that kind of trip. It was more of a tradition. Gudrun thought it was a pointless expense, although Troy guessed that she was unhappy that he had gone without her and met a beautiful film star. But she had a nice friendly way about her, which hid, up to a point, how argumentative she was. She would press home a point constantly, almost as if she knew that at some juncture, Troy would simply let it go. Then she would find another and off they would go again. And yet he was strangely drawn to her. On the way back, she broached another subject.

'Why don't you move in with me? That flat of yours is like an old railway signal box and it's the same rent as mine. We might as well pay the same rent between us and live somewhere presentable.'

'You seem to think every aspect of my life is a needless expense. I hope I never need brain surgery while I'm with you.'

'That's how you seem to live. You won't be young forever.'

'That's what they said to Dorian Gray.'

She ignored this.

'It would make so much sense.'

'It's too soon. I'll think about it.'

Nonetheless, he stayed the night with her. It was nearby and it was a nice pad. Not as nice as Shirley's had been – he was still comparing everything with Shirley, even after all this time – but after a few days of her charming and smiling persistence, he agreed that it made sense. It made sense financially, although not as much as it would have done if they had bought a place together. But it was way too soon to be thinking of that. No doubt that was the next stage in her plan. And so, for the moment, this was the plan that made sense. He moved in.

It was many weeks after the party that Gloria ran into Barry Keeler again. It was in an 'A' list restaurant. She was having dinner with her manager, who rejoiced in the name Lassie Koruba, when he came over to talk to her.

'Hello again, Gloria, if I may call you that.'

She seemed pleased to see him. And she noted that he knew Lassie as well. He seemed very well connected here in the ghastly city of fallen angels. Or did Lassie just know *of* him? You can't tell in LA by the way people talk to each other. So, Keeler was a known commodity. And if somebody else knows somebody then we immediately assume that they must be reasonable and decent people. Naturally, when Keeler asked both ladies to join him at his table (and presumably at his expense) it seemed a normal thing to do.

Keeler was a charming and witty host and he insisted to the waiter that the bill would be for him. Not many people do that when lunching with celebrities.

It had been a long time now since Gloria had lost Leonard. The pain was still there but it had been somewhat blunted by her busy life and the necessity to keep together for Melinda. She had not dated anyone in that period. Unlike Shirley, she could not separate love and sex. It seemed not unreasonable that she was entitled to start dating at some time. She was still young and ravishing. Time was not likely to allow her to get more young and beautiful – and the clock ticks much more loudly for actresses and glamorous film stars than it does for others. So, when Lassie excused herself and went to the powder room, as she quaintly called it, Keeler asked Gloria if he could call her sometime. She said yes and gave him her number, which she very rarely gave out to anyone who was not a professional contact.

He duly called about 48 hours later and they arranged to have dinner. It wasn't easy for Gloria to find a window, but dinner with a top casting agent fell through one night, so she was able to fit him in. The chances are she would have found an opportunity to see him anyway, as she was quite taken with him.

Keeler picked her up in his Rolls Royce three nights after calling her. They went to a new restaurant. Keeler knew a lot of people in this place too. He knew the man who ran the valet parking, he knew the greeter and he knew the maitre d'. Gloria asked him if he knew the people who caught the lobster and he laughed easily.

'I know a lot of people. It's my job.'

She decided not to interrogate him about that until they had settled in at their table and ordered.

'I haven't been on a date for a long while,' she told him, once they had had their first drinks. And then, she realised that she wasn't sure that it *was* a date. After all, while she may have been a Holy Grail for most red-blooded men, there were plenty of other reasons why a hot celebrity would be courted by a man – usually to do with finance or connections. Sex is not always a priority with highly motivated men. Often, they take it for granted as a by-product of their routine machinations, like the other benefits on an expense account. Keeler's reply was disarmingly easy.

'That's no problem. Let's just look upon it as two nice people having a pleasant evening out. If more happens, then we'll think ourselves lucky.'

'You're not one of these men who says, *You make your own luck?*'

'Not exactly; but preparation leads to luck. Or as Kissinger put it, *Luck is the residue of design.* But there are other versions of the same aphorism.'

She smiled at him. He clearly didn't trade in superficial chat-up lines.

'Tell me about your work. Do you have a lot of celebrity clients?'

'Sure. Creative people are not always...what can I say...?'

'Stable people?'

'Let's say that they are less likely to drive in the slow lane. Their whole life is risk and challenge. And an extraordinary life means extraordinary stresses.'

'That's where you come in.'

'That's where I'm privileged to help.'

'In what way?'

'All sorts of ways. People are different and therefore the solutions and methods we use to help them are different.'

And so on. It all seemed very smooth and reassuring, but also a little vague. Pretenders are best exposed by pinning them down on details, but this was a social occasion, and so far Keeler had done nothing to upset her or arouse her suspicions.

He smiled and said, 'I'm glad you're curious'. But he added nothing else. After the meal, which was pleasant verging on romantic, he took her home. He understood perfectly that she couldn't invite him in – because of Melinda. She agreed to a second date.

It was only on this second date that he asked her to come to one of his 'sessions'. Lassie would be there and perhaps 'some others you might know'.

'They are all well connected people,' he explained.

She said that she was pretty busy and he replied, 'So is everyone else I meet. Professionally and socially. In fact, it's because of those busy lives that they ask me for my help.'

Then he smiled and added, 'But some people also like me'.

She smiled too and said that she would love to come but not for a couple of weeks. She really did have a lot on.

CHAPTER TWENTY-NINE

Gudrun and Troy were mooching about in Islington one weekend when they ran into Ted Gosworth. Gosworth was an actor like Troy. Or rather, not like Troy since, whereas Troy was constantly engaged in acting roles and other work, Ted was permanently resting. Why this was, was something of a mystery, since Ted had all the qualities, fixtures and fittings necessary to make a good success of life. He was effortlessly charming, good-looking and intelligent and had a great sense of humour. Perhaps he was only playing at it, since he was one of those roguish characters who cruise through life at other people's expense. Troy was glad to meet him because he owed him some money.

'Haven't forgotten about it, matey,' said Gosworth breezily, slapping Troy on the shoulder. 'Get it back to you shortly.'

That was the great thing about Gosworth: if you lent him money, he never forgot about it. Troy introduced him to Gudrun who gave him her nicest smile. Troy wondered if she would nag Gosworth about his finances. Gosworth said it was great to see them both and invited them for a drink in a nearby pub. Troy said they were in a hurry, since he knew that if Gosworth didn't have his money, then he probably wouldn't have enough to buy a round of drinks. But Gudrun said,

'We're not in a hurry at all. We're just looking around and having a walk. And I could do with a drink.'

So they popped into the Slug and Lettuce halfway up Upper Street. People like Ted Gosworth are subtle. He had enough money for the first round and then naturally steered the conversation around to the imminent explosion of good fortune in his dormant dramatic career.

'It's a really exciting opportunity,' he was saying, as they stood at the bar and sipped their drinks. 'All expenses paid tour of Asia with the Mercia Shakespeare Company. Three months! Can't be bad, eh? The guy told me I was a shoo-in for the part of Tybalt in *Romeo and Juliet*. And I'll be understudying for Hamlet.'

Troy smiled tightly, but Gudrun beamed and nodded as if this were the great news she had been expecting all her life. Troy had been here before - like when Gosworth had two commercials coming up which were a dead cert. Troy had lent him the hundred pounds on the back of this certainty, but had seen neither a penny of it back nor an advert on television in which Gosworth had featured.

'It sounds very exciting,' said Gudrun, who had no previous knowledge of him. Troy had had no time to warn her, so she pitched in by buying the next round.

'It is if it comes off,' Troy said, desperately trying to stop her getting too excited. After all, he didn't want her to lend him any money. And she seemed very taken with him, as women always were.

'Don't be such a misery,' she told Troy. 'It sounds wonderful.'

'Oh, it is, it is.'

But Gosworth had a bigger surprise in store.

'It'll be great, if I can just survive the next two weeks until the tour starts.'

'Oh, is it as soon as that?' asked Gudrun.

All the cold, technocratic analysis which she usually brought to Troy's affairs had disappeared completely now. She was like a debutante meeting royalty.

'Yes, but the sticky point is, I've just split up with my girlfriend.'

Troy and Gudrun were both very sorry to hear that. They both said so. Gudrun looked as if she meant it.

'Yeah, it's a bit of a downer. I've got to move out of her place and there's not much point in getting another pad right now as the tour starts in two or three weeks. I just need somewhere to crash down for a few days until we're off to exotic Japan.'

Troy was in like a flash.

'Well, I hope you get sorted soon. We're a bit pushed for space at the moment. Sorry we can't help.'

'We're not pushed for space at all,' said Gudrun. 'We've got a spare room.'

'No, we haven't: it's all full of my stuff.'

'Which I've been asking you to clear up for ages. You can do it tonight. It won't hurt for a couple of weeks.'

'Four at the most,' said Gosworth, helpfully.

Troy noticed he hadn't made any mention of rent.

'When are we talking about for this tour, exactly?' he asked. But Gosworth had his answer ready. His type always does.

'Haven't got an exact date yet. You know what it's like with these international events. It's a question of keeping all the balls in the air.'

Smooth as baby oil.

Gudrun recovered some of her questioning temperament.

'And this tour, it is bona fide? It won't fall through?'

'Oh, absolutely. All done and dusted. Just waiting for the off date. They'll get back to me this week.'

He peered playfully at his empty glass. 'Are we er...?'

Troy bought another round. Gosworth had a double scotch and ginger this time.

'Cheers,' he said. 'Lucky meeting you two.'

'Lucky isn't the word,' said Troy.

And of course, as a bonus, Gosworth would make sure he sent Troy his money on the first pay date. That meant he had a vested interest in making sure Gosworth got to the Far East in one piece.

'You'll put me at the top of the list, won't you?' said Troy drily.

'Surely, matey, surely.'

When it became clear that nobody would be buying any more drinks, Gudrun and Troy left after giving Gosworth their address. He said he would be round in a day or so, as if he were promising a treat for them. He couldn't tell them how grateful he was.

As they walked back to the flat, Gudrun said,

'Why didn't you want to help your friend?'

'You don't know him. He's always in trouble.'

'Well, he seems to have fallen on his feet now.'

'Yes – meeting us.'

'Well, he's got a good opportunity, so he must be a good risk.'

'If he's telling the truth.'

'Well, if he's a liar, why is he your friend? Why did you have a drink with him?'

'Because you insisted...oh never mind. I was hoping he'd have the hundred pounds.'

'A hundred pounds? Is that all? You little meanie,' she said as she tickled him playfully. 'It's not like you need the money.'

'No, but it's not like I gave it to him as a present for being a good boy. And he's probably got fifty creditors like me after him.'

'Well, I thought he seemed very nice.'

'Of course he does! That's why people lend him money which they never see again. And in certain special cases, usually women, they then lend him even more.'

'Well, he's bound to pay you now that you've offered to help him out. He will put you at the top of the list.'

'Oh, certainly! The list is marked *Extra Special Suckers I Can Tap Three or Four Times*. And anyway, it was you who offered to help him out.'

He reminded her that the Shakespeare tour of Asia – the Mercia Shakespeare Company? Who the hell were they? – was probably all spaghetti.

'Spaghetti? You do say the strangest things.'

They went home. Gosworth moved in at the weekend. He seemed to have rather a lot of stuff.

CHAPTER THIRTY

'What exactly,' asked Gloria, 'is a séance for the living?'

She and Keeler were driving to their fourth date and Keeler had promised something quite unusual. They arrived at a large private house which clearly belonged to mid-range wealthy people rather than top rank celebrities like Gloria. They would have good security, but only sufficient to deal with burglars rather than deranged fans and other stalkers.

'A séance is when you try to contact the dead who have been lost to you.'

'I don't like all that stuff: it freaks me out.'

'Sure, I understand. In fact, neither do I. But what I have created is a meeting in which we try to recover the spirits of those we have lost, not to death but to life.'

'It sounds intriguing,' she said as they got out of the car and walked to the front door.

They pressed the bell and were admitted by a sombre butler who may have been from the Philippines. Inside, the living room was precisely what you might have expected to see in a real séance – if there is any such thing. There were heavy curtains covering the windows. There was also a number of chairs set in a circle – except that there was no table in between them. All but two chairs were occupied, which suggested invitation-only rather than pay-on-entry. Lassie was sitting on one of the chairs.

The room was brightly lit and, as they sat down, nobody suggested that the lights be switched off. Clearly, there were to be no theatrics, mirrors, reflectors, pyrotechnics, ventriloquial utterances or any of the other cheap gimmicks associated with the average séance. Gloria wanted to make a joke about musical chairs, but she had promised Keeler that she would take it seriously.

'So what happens?' she whispered.

'Please, there is no need to whisper,' said a corpulent, middle-aged, bearded man. 'This isn't some magical charade. We're here for a serious purpose and part of that purpose is clear communication.'

'I'm so sorry.'

'That's quite all right,' replied the man. 'No criticism was intended. We just want you to relax and be yourself.'

'We certainly do,' added Keeler. 'We're not here to draw up the past but to increase our sensitivity for the present.'

'But do we join hands?' said a small woman with closely cropped red hair. Obviously, Gloria was not the only newcomer.

'We can,' said Keeler. 'We can if it helps. There are no hard and fast rules about what we do or don't do.'

He began to take charge.

'We're here tonight to communicate with the living. Some of you know each other and some of you are strangers. But we can leave knowing more about each other and about ourselves. Now, let's be humorously theatrical and say, "Is there anybody there?"'

'Yes, I'm here,' said Lassie.

'And do you have a message for anyone here tonight?'

'Yes,' said Lassie, 'I have a message for Mr Bradbury.'

Bradbury turned out to be the man with the beard. He thanked her for her interest and said he would be delighted to hear the message.

'We met a couple of months ago. Three sessions ago, it was. I disliked you but didn't say so. I behaved insincerely and may have affected the atmosphere. I would like to make it right.'

'Consider it righted,' said the man called Bradbury, nodding and smiling.

'Thank you for your warmth and understanding,' replied Lassie. 'I feel we are much closer.'

'We are closer,' he said.

'Anything else?' asked Keeler.

There was a pause. Then a small, bald, mousey looking man said,

'Yes, I have a message for Miss Greatorex.'

'And what is your message?' asked Keeler.

'Firstly, thank you for coming here tonight with an open mind.'

'Well, I hope I have…', said Gloria, but Keeler lifted a finger to ask her to remain silent while the man was talking. Gloria was glad because she felt embarrassed. She wasn't actually sure that she had come with an open mind. She wasn't even sure that she had one now and she didn't really want to hear any messages.

'And secondly,' said the small man, 'I wish to tell you that your success will continue if you believe in yourself.'

'Erm…thank you for your good wishes. May I ask how you know this?'

She expected some talk about auras and vibrations, but the man astonished her by simply shrugging.

Keeler spoke: 'Miss Greatorex has come here tonight in the spirit of enquiry. She has seen what we have to offer - which is the liberating spirit of complete openness.'

A few more messages were exchanged, then the meeting broke up. To Gloria's relief, it was not followed by a drug-crazed orgy or even a drink-up. There was a buffet in the next room where they all chatted for a while until, one-by-one, they drifted off. Eventually, the only one left, apart from herself and Keeler, was the corpulent bearded man. Gloria guessed that it was his house. It was definitely too small for Keeler.

They both thanked him for his hospitality and took their leave.

On the drive back, he naturally asked her what she thought of it.

'Well...it was...interesting.'

Keeler laughed.

'You thought no such thing. You thought it was a fatuous waste of time.'

'How do you know what I thought?'

'That was the purpose of the evening. It's the whole purpose of my philosophy which is to get people's real feelings to the surface. I was watching you very carefully.'

She was bewildered; but she was at least impressed by the fact that he didn't mind that she hadn't liked it.

'Some people find it liberating; some don't.'

He looked at her and smiled.

'Maybe it's not a British thing. I mean talking about your innermost self.'

She laughed.

'It most definitely isn't a British thing.'

Then he asked if she wanted to continue seeing him. She said yes. This time, when he dropped her off at her house, he leaned over and kissed her. She let him.

CHAPTER THIRTY-ONE

Ted Gosworth made himself right at home. He wasn't so anti-social as to keep to his room. He sat on the sofa and watched television with them, with his feet up on the coffee table. He sat in between Gudrun and Troy. Troy got so annoyed that he offered Gosworth a few quid if he would go out for a drink.

'Nice of you to offer, matey, but I need to keep all my pennies for the Asia trip.'

So Troy had to lend him the few quid anyway, which Gosworth pocketed.

'Oh, yes, the Asia trip. Any news on that? Like a leaving date, maybe?'

'No, not yet. I'll give them a call tomorrow. Chivvy them along a bit. This is boring. Shall we watch a film?'

And he changed the channel.

Two to three weeks, four at the most, soon became six, seven and then ten. Troy began to reckon it in months. But when he tried to challenge Gosworth on the issue, not only did Gudrun fail to back him up, but she said,

'Oh, Troy, stop nagging him. It's not his fault.'

No-one mentioned the tour again, but Gosworth had some great news about a new job in the West with the Bristol Repertory Company. He was very excited about it.

'Sounds just the lollipop,' he said jovially, as he said everything. 'And then I'll be able to stop bothering you.'

'Oh, you're not bothering us, Ted,' said Gudrun. 'Don't be silly.'

Troy didn't think he was being silly. On the contrary, it was the first welcome statement he had heard from Gosworth.

After three months, with Asia completely forgotten and the Bristol Rep job also turning out to be another mirage, Troy had to take stock. His options were obvious, but none was particularly palatable. The first was to say to Gudrun, *either he goes, or I go*. But truthfully, this would be a bluff. And moreover, it was a bluff that Gudrun, judging by recent form, might well call. If she did, then he would be in the same position that Gosworth had been in, while Gosworth would be in clover. The second was to go up to him and tell him to his face to get out. That would mean that he would either start whining that he had nowhere to go (if Gudrun was present) or maybe get violent with Troy if she wasn't. He wasn't much bigger than Troy, but he had a very unsettling air of confidence. And Troy wasn't a hundred per cent certain that Gosworth wasn't a bit unstable. The next option was to simply quietly go at a time most convenient to himself. That would mean abandoning Gudrun. He damned himself for a coward for not taking any steps at all. And he was secretly furious at her: she had got him into this mess and refused to help resolve it.

One day, after Gosworth had been their house guest for four months, Troy had a particularly busy day in town. He had a lot of voiceovers to do in the morning for Capital Radio and then a meeting with his agent. Working on the principle that a busy man gets things done, he vowed to make the decision that day.

After he had finished recording his commercials, he wandered over to the agency. He still belonged to the same company, but his original agent, Percy, had moved on to the great drying-out clinic in the sky. His new contact was called Niamh Sullivan. She seemed to know what she was doing. In an auspicious move, she met him in the office rather than in the pub across the road, an arrangement which promised great things.

Niamh was a portly but pretty Irish woman with a pushy, no-nonsense attitude. A bit like a red-headed Diana Dors from Donegal, if you go back that far. A pushy character is no drawback in the world of showbiz agents, so Troy was happy with her and she was happy with him. She had trained as a lawyer and had once gone round the office singing, 'A verbal contract is like a melody'. She said 'thanks a million' a lot, even when people hadn't done anything for her.

'You're getting to be one of the best voiceovers in the country,' she told him. Troy had used another agency called *Calypso* to get voiceovers, but Niamh had usurped their function. She had more contacts and Troy now had all his affairs under one roof, which was miles better. Gudrun had approved of this.

'That's great stuff, Niamh. And I really appreciate what you're pulling in for me, but the trouble with voiceovers is that they're so anonymous. Is there...you know...something a bit more visible?'

'Darling, we have to take what we're given in life.'

This was an odd thing for an agent to say, but he nodded understandingly.

'All I'm asking is to have a look around. Put me about for other things. I've got a lot to offer, not just my voice. I'm getting, well...sort of buried.'

'Oh, rubbish. Look at Miriam Margolyes, the queen of the voiceovers. You wouldn't describe her as obscure, would you?'

'No, unfortunately not; but I'm just not getting anything else.'

'Look, Troy, you're making money and we're making money out of you.'

'Yes, but it's getting harder and harder to get real acting work because nobody has heard of me.'

'Do you want to be a robot on kids' TV again?'

'Why not? It was a good living. And I was known. Not like Prince Charles is known, but producers knew me.'

Niamh laughed. She knew this was a complete reversal of his original view of the job.

'Do you know, of all the actors I've ever known, you're the only one I ever thought wasn't driven by ego? Looks like I was wrong.'

They both laughed.

'Anyway, you hated being Rumpledine.'

'Only while I was doing it. Afterwards, I felt an indescribable nostalgia for when life was simple. I pine for the days of innocent entertainment.'

'Yes, well, I shall remain vigilant on your behalf.'

'Do what you can, Niamh.'

'I will, darling. Thanks a million. Be lucky.'

'Somebody's got to be, but it isn't anyone I know.'

He left the agency and walked to the station. Then he realised that he only had about twenty pounds on him, so he went to the cash machine. He put in his card and waited for the cash to come out. But all he got was a message saying, *We cannot process this transaction. Please contact your bank.*

He assumed that this was a problem with the cash machine, so he moved to the one next to it and received the same message. Then he reinserted his card and checked his balance. Zero. He should have had £5000 in it: there was nothing. He panicked and tried his other account with the Building Society. There should have been £10,000 in that. No, there wasn't: there was zero. He had nothing. Both accounts could not be wrong - unless there was some kind of nationwide meltdown with the system. But no, a man was just withdrawing some cash from the first machine. Troy could see from his card that he was with the same building society.

There was a conclusion to be leaped to here, but Troy seemed to be incapable of doing any intellectual leaping. He was completely numb. Unlike Shirley, he had never blasphemously claimed that bad things only happened to other people; and yet, he realised in a moment of awakening that he had always secretly thought that, without knowing or saying it. He ran to the tube station in terror. The train didn't carry him back home nearly as quickly as he willed it to. He ran all the way to the flat and burst through the door like an actor in a bad cop movie.

'Hello!' he shouted. But he knew no-one would answer. Gudrun was gone. Gosworth was gone. Gosworth's stuff was gone. The flat had been rented, but presumably the furniture had been hers because most of that was gone too. They had planned this to an exquisite degree. Gudrun had had access to all his accounts and she had cleaned him out. But he suspected that Gosworth, the vile seducer, had been the instigator of this betrayal. He sat down on the floor and began to shake. They hadn't even left him a few pounds to help him survive. That was the biggest outrage. Taking a quick stock, he remembered that the rent was paid up for three weeks. They had missed a trick there. And at least he still had his credit cards.

Or did he?

He ran out of the flat and down to the shopping precinct. He found a cash machine and put one of his credit cards in. One of them had a limit of £5000 and the other £3000. He had used up about a third of it. But no. Both cards were now right up to the limit. They had probably drawn out the balance in cash. She must have passed Gosworth the cards while he was asleep. Both were now useless. But not only that – he would have to pay it all back himself or watch his credit rating sink into the sea. Gudrun and Gosworth had ripped him off to the tune of about twenty-one thousand pounds. This was the first time in his life that he had been in such an appalling fix, and there was little or nothing he could do. He couldn't think of anyone who could help him. His parents had been divorced and poor. Most of his friends were jobbing actors who lived from hand to mouth. His agent? He had more chance of getting the teeth out of a basilisk. He was in a dreadful fix.

By a curious omission, they had not taken his PC from the desk. They had only taken their own stuff. Perhaps they thought it could be traced. He could sell that. But what the hell else could he do?

CHAPTER THIRTY-TWO

March 12th, 2012, was Gloria's birthday. She was thirty. It was supposed to be one of those milestone celebrations. She was still young, but the damage wrought by time was all the more deadly for being incremental.

Keeler threw a party for her. It was a lavish affair held at a hired beach house. Keeler never mentioned whose house it was. Everybody who was anybody was there. Troy, not being a Los Angeles somebody, had not been invited. He read about it online. Not that he felt snubbed: it was probably a surprise party organised by professionals who had never heard of their own grandmothers because they weren't famous.

Not that Troy could have offered to go. Going to the shops was a challenge at the moment. He boxed up his PC and walked it down to the Cash Converters at the bottom of the high street. He got some money for it and the option of redeeming it if his luck changed from unbearable to just terrible. His luck would need a very big pivot to change that much. Now, he had no immediate access to emails, and communication would be crucial to the next steps. He went to the bank and told them what happened. They told him to report it to the police so he could get an incident number. He hoped Gloria was having more fun. He tried calling her several times and got neither a reply nor a call back. Still, Gloria was, he knew very well, very busy.

Gloria and Melinda arrived at the party under a pretext but, as is always the case with surprise parties, she had guessed what was happening.

She received a rapturous round of applause as she entered. Melinda looked excited. This was her first big night out in a proper party dress. They both went round the guests – working the room, as it is known – thanking everybody personally.

'Mom, who were those people?' asked Melinda.

'I have no idea, darling. I don't know half the people here.'

After everyone had relaxed and had a few drinks, Keeler got up and made the inevitable speech. He was the kind of man who got up and made speeches. He probably would have made a speech after a car crash.

'Can we have our special lady up here, please?'

Gloria obediently came to the front, whereupon Keeler presented her with gifts from various people. The crowd applauded each present, usually from someone she had never met. Somebody asked, 'Where's your gift, Barry?'

'Oh, I've saved the best until last,' replied Keeler, who was never at a loss for words, even if he was a stranger to originality. 'May I present my friend, Mr Khan.'

He gestured to the crowd and a tall, handsome turbaned Sikh man emerged. He was resplendent in traditional coloured frock coat, so it was surprising that nobody had seen him come in.

'Is he my present?' said Gloria, and everyone laughed.

'I'd like you all to meet my good friend, Mr Khan,' said Keeler. He seemed to have so many friends. Mr Khan bowed elegantly but did not smile.

'He is here to present you with my gift – your personal birthday star chart.'

Everyone *oohed* and *aahed* as if they had rehearsed it and Gloria looked delighted and intrigued, as if pleasantly surprised after expecting a set of Tupperware salad bowls.

'Here? In front of everyone?' she asked.

'No, no. Not at all. We'll go into the study while the guests enjoy themselves.'

And so Keeler, Gloria and Khan repaired to a side room. If it was a study, then there was plenty of room for people to do the studying. It was like the reading room at the British Museum. It contained a large table with chairs. They all sat. Mr Khan placed a leather document case on the table.

'Mr Khan predicted the 9/11 disaster.'

The eponymous stargazer nodded his head to accept the tribute. Although not a natural cynic, Gloria knew that you could fill Wembley Stadium with all the people who claim to have predicted the World Trade Centre tragedy. (And Lord's Cricket Ground with the ones who had predicted Princess Diana's death.) But this was a special present on her birthday, so she did not want to be a spoilsport. And she did think that it might be interesting.

'How impressive,' she said.

Mr Khan spoke at last, in the quiet voice of an educated Empire Indian.

'May I ask the time of your birth?'

Gloria said that she had no idea.

'I'm so sorry, I wasn't prepared. I assume it was early in the morning because they always are. But I don't know.'

'It really doesn't matter. It could help but it is not vital.'

He asked her about her family and her career. Gloria was a little disappointed. She was under the impression that *he* was going to tell *her* things. Instead, it seemed to be an irritating interrogation. Keeler must have sensed her disappointment because he said, 'Be patient, Gloria. Mr Khan wants to tell you the future, not the past.'

Khan then produced some charts from the little document holder. They appeared to have astrological cyphers on them. He studied them and said nothing for a while. Gloria hoped Keeler would not suspect that she was a bit irritated. Then finally, Khan spoke.

'I sense a great deal of pain - but you do not speak of it. You are holding it in. You are courageous, so courageous. You are being strong for your daughter, are you not?'

Gloria must have looked annoyed because Keeler said,

'I didn't tell him that. This has not been in any way prepared.'

'I believe you, Barry.'

Well, why shouldn't she? Her private life was quite in the public domain. Mr Khan could have read that much in the papers.

'This pain,' continued Khan, 'will not go away without being addressed.'
His quiet voice began to build in intensity.

'The pain will not go away. You think that time will cure it, but you are mistaken. Your grief is growing inside of you. It is building to the point where it will reach a crisis. You know this - and in knowing this you are complicit in your own agony.'

Gloria could hardly deny any of this. Tears formed in her eyes.

'You must break with the past. A good, clean cut of the axe. Break with your entire past. Look only to the future, otherwise, you will suffer a severe emotional implosion.'

Gloria broke down sobbing.

'Is this your idea of a birthday present?' she said.

'Mr Keeler did not know what I would say. But you must understand Miss Gloria, this is just your first step towards release. You must move on and forget all the shadows of the past which come to haunt you at night, when no-one is watching.'

Gloria stood up.

'Yes, thank you, I will. And now, if you don't mind, Barry, I would like to go home.'

Keeler also stood up.

'Gloria, I am so sorry. I truly didn't know what Mr Khan would say. Please accept my apologies.'

'There's no need for apologies. Melinda and I really must go now.'

'Of course, whatever you say. But please try to remember – tonight, you have taken the first steps towards your liberation from your agony.'

'Yes, I'm sure. Can you ask Melinda to come in here, please?'

'I'll explain everything to the guests.'

Keeler went to fetch Melinda while Gloria left by a different exit. They met at the front of the house.

'Mom, are you all right?'

'Yes, I'm fine, sweetheart. Just a little tired. Barry will take us both home now. I have to be up early tomorrow.'

'But you said you didn't have to be up tomorrow.'

'Mummy made a mistake.'

After they arrived home, Melinda was met at the door by Mrs K. Gloria said to Melinda,

'Go to bed, darling. I'll be a few minutes.'

'OK mom. Are you sure you're all right?'

'Yes, I'm really fine. You go off. I'll be in soon.'

After Melinda had gone inside, Gloria said to Keeler:

'Actually, I'm not at all tired.'

'Would you like to go for a drive?'

'Why not? Not too far.'

Keeler drove them around for a while as they talked.

'I suppose that Mr Khan was right about one thing: I am bottling up this pain.'

'He usually is right. I know this wasn't what you expected for a birthday celebration, but you have to believe me when I say it was probably for the best. I've helped and healed many people just by liberating what they were clamping down in the pressure cooker of their souls.'

They passed a beautiful mansion.

'That's a nice house.'

'I'm glad you think so: it's mine. You haven't seen it yet. Do you want to take a look?'

'Yes, I'd love to see it.'

He pressed a switch on the dashboard and the electronic gates of the house opened. They drove in.

CHAPTER THIRTY-THREE

The police took some details from Troy and said they would look into it. He realised with horror and a considerable amount of shame, that he knew almost nothing about Gudrun. And necessarily much less about Ted Gosworth.

'And this man Gosworth was an actor?' asked the emaciated and childlike constable who interviewed him.

'Well, that was the occupation he gave the jobcentre. Actually, he's been resting for so long he's almost catatonic.'

'What was the last job he had? Do you know?'

'I've no idea. He'd be ideal as one of those statue performance artists. Anything where you don't have to do much moving around.'

'Well, he's certainly on the move now.'

'Yes, I have to give him that. He certainly shifted very sharpish while I was out.'

'How did you get to know him?'

'The same way you always get to know such people. A friend of a friend of a friend. All of them think he's recommended by the other friends. I think I need fewer friends. Remind me to come off Facebook.'

'And this woman...'

The young and innocent policeman took a deep breath and then plunged recklessly into the name.

'...Good Run Googlen Bicker'

'A very courageous and worthy attempt.'

'Thank you. Sounds like a sort of automatic machine pistol. How well did you know her?'

'What can I say? She was my girlfriend. Somehow we never got round to discussing previous convictions over those romantic candlelit dinners.'

'Any previous address for this Gosworth?' asked the constable.

'You're kidding. When they bury him, it'll be temporarily in somebody else's grave.'

After he left the police station, he went to the accountancy firm where he had met Gudrun. No, they knew nothing of her. She had been a temp sent by an agency. She had been filling in for someone on maternity leave. Her husband? No, we were under the impression that she was unmarried. But they weren't sure.

Troy left feeling an unmitigated nitwit. He found what was probably the last internet café in London and fired off an email to Gloria. He had called her repeatedly but had had no reply. Then he had a brainwave. It was a little manipulative, but he was desperate. He sent an email to Melinda asking her to get her mother to call him. It was urgent.

After that, he went to the bank and opened a new account. He sent the new details to Niamh and, by the Grace of God, he received some outstanding payments for his voiceovers. Never had he been so glad of the show business agents' legendarily tight-fisted practice of sitting on payments until the last minute. If they had paid him when they should, he would have lost it with the rest. It wasn't a fortune but a welcome respite. He could pay the rent for the next month and buy some food. But he heard nothing from Gloria.

Gloria was used to comfort and wealth. Not that she was self-indulgent, but she had, or could have, anything she wanted. But she awoke in the largest and most luxurious bed she had ever seen in her life. She was startled for a moment. She hadn't slept anywhere except her own bed for years, wherever in the world she was. She reached over and touched Keeler's naked body. Now she knew where she was.

'Barry, are you awake?'

'Yes. What time is it?'

'It's early. I couldn't sleep.'

He raised himself up to look at the radio alarm. It was only five thirty. He rolled over and kissed her.

'Now my life is complete,' he said.

She smiled.

'You do flatter.'

'No, I don't. I never do. My whole life's work is getting to the truth that people suppress. They normally discover that suppressing it is more painful than releasing it.'

'I'm sorry it's early, but I do have to go.'

'Not a problem. I'm usually up at 6.00am anyway. I can run you home and then hit the training room.'

He got out of bed. He certainly wasn't lying about working out. She could see his perfect physique. She got up herself and reminded him that she had a body that no gymnasium or fitness regime could create. Exercise could keep it in trim, but the original creation was a miracle straight from God. In the past, she had always been careful not to abuse His gift. They both got dressed.

'Oh, by the way,' he said, as if it were nothing, 'if you're having difficulty sleeping, you might try one of these.'

He tossed her a small box. She read the label.

Herbal Sleep Remedy. The natural way to go to bed and wake up relaxed.

They looked harmless enough. She put them in her handbag. Then they walked down to the garage and he drove her home. She arrived before Melinda or Mrs K had risen, which was what she had wanted.

A couple of days later, Troy received a reply from Melinda. She had a new phone number. He sent back a response saying she could call him at any time at all but that he couldn't afford to call anyone. She phoned him within the hour while he was eating some chips from a polystyrene carton.

'Hello Uncle Troy. Are you OK?'

'I'm fine sweetheart. How's your mum?'

'She's OK. I think she's tired.'

Troy was alerted by her tone.

'Tell me what's on your mind, Melinda.'

'She's got a boyfriend.'

'Go on.'

There was a silence.

'You don't like him?'

'Not really.'

'Is he horrible to you?'

'No, he's really nice. And he's nice to mom. But I don't like him.'

Troy was puzzled. Children often have good instincts about people; they haven't learned to dissemble yet. But it might just have been the routine jealousy of a young girl who had lost one parent and didn't want to lose another to someone else. Melinda was at a critical age.

'Listen, Melinda: whatever happens, I'm here. I want you to remember that. If there's a problem, I'm your friend, OK?'

'Yes. Are you coming over?'

'I can't. Not unless your mother calls me back.'

'Are you poor?'

'Well, yes, frankly love, I'm too poor.'

'I'll tell her to call you.'

'Is Mrs K looking after you?'

'Oh yes.'

That was good. That lugubrious Polish she-bear would tear anyone to pieces if they tried to hurt Melinda.

'I'll speak to you soon.'

'Goodbye.'

About ten days later, Troy received an official-looking letter from the United States. It was a cheque for three thousand pounds. Troy hadn't seen a cheque for a while. Very few people sent them these days and it was probably the last one he would ever see. It was drawn on the account of an attorney at law in Los Angeles. He gathered that it had been sent on the instructions of Gloria. But there was no note except a terse line or two saying that they had been instructed by their client to send this payment.

Troy was overjoyed and felt a relaxing fizz of relief along his nervous system. But he was saddened that there was no note. No message, no card, no phone call warning him it would be arriving and to call as soon as he received it to confirm receipt. Nothing. That wasn't like Gloria. But there again, it *would* be like her to be generous without fanfare. He tried to call her. This time there was a message saying, *The number you have dialled is not in service.* Obviously, she had either lost her phone or changed the number for a less clear purpose.

He called Melinda but she went straight to voicemail. He left a message thanking her for her help, telling her to thank Gloria and reminding her that if she needed anything, she was to get in touch with him and he would swim across the Atlantic to help her. Then he walked all the way down to Cash Converters and liberated his computer.

Gloria had nothing particularly that she had to do that day (for a change), so she could spend it with Melinda. That was a day well spent for her. They went to a health spa to be pampered. This meant lying about on divans while various gooey things were rubbed on them.

'Uncle Troy said thank you for the money.'

'Well, I wouldn't want him to be in trouble. I knew he wouldn't have asked if he hadn't needed it.'

'Will you call him? He's very grateful. He says your number has changed.'

'Well, no; if he's in touch with you, that's fine.' And then she added, 'We must look to the future now, not to the past.'

'Why?'

'Because it's lost, darling. You've got your whole life to think of. That's the important thing.'

A woman in a white coat dress scraped something browny-green from a large bowl and began to apply it to Gloria's body.

'What is this?'

'It contains all the rich nutrients from the ocean,' said the woman.

It looked and smelled like something from the bottom of a blocked sewer. Then as an extra special recommendation, the attendant said, 'It's very expensive.'

'Yes, I bet it is.'

'Mommy, what's it like to be poor?'

'I don't know, sweetheart - and if I have anything to do with it, neither will you.'

They both had a beautiful relaxing day, but when Gloria went to bed that night, she felt stressed and tired. She had an early start in the morning and needed to sleep. She tossed and turned for a bit. Then she remembered the herbal tablets Keeler had given her. They would probably be useless, like most herbal remedies, but it was worth a try. She went to the ensuite bathroom for some water and then swallowed two of the tablets. She went back to bed and that was the last thing she could recall. She awoke at 7.00am the next morning. She had had the best night's sleep in a long age and felt fully relaxed. Those herbal tablets were just the job, she thought. In fact, they were so effective that she checked on the pack to make sure that that was all they were. She was satisfied by the blurb. They contained no unnatural substances or chemical additives, it said.

CHAPTER THIRTY-FOUR

Troy was back in business again, thanks to Gloria's generosity. His only problem was that he'd wanted to thank his friend for her help, but he couldn't get through. It was curious: the closer he got to Melinda, the more estranged he became from her mother. It riled and upset him. She was his friend - and far more than that: they were united by powerful bonds, not the least of which was the fact that they had both lost loved ones, who had also been close friends, in tragic circumstances. And that was before you came to consider how they had met. He had no way of knowing about the forces which were drawing them apart.

However, his main concern now was to get enough work to pay her back. Three thousand pounds to Gloria was like Troy putting a pound in a tramp's coffee cup. But it was the thought that counted, and he was determined to repay her. He was all the more determined to repay the loan because she didn't need the money. That would be taking advantage and he was no Ted Gosworth. And if she refused it, well, he would give it to charity.

These reflections led him down another path: namely, what the hell was he going to do with the rest of his life? Acting, if you were very lucky, was a good way of living. He earned good money, even if it had been stolen. And he might do again. Or he might not. He was over thirty now. If he wanted to change career, then he would have to start thinking about it. Acting was not only a precarious way to make a living, but he wasn't actually doing anything that might properly be called acting. Not as he understood the word. He wasn't being challenged, he wasn't making producers think twice about a role, he wasn't well known or respected and he wasn't going to draw in the crowds for a year with his revolutionary *King Lear* at the Globe. Even worse, he wasn't even playing Inspector Mendicott in *Death Wears Corsets* at the Scunthorpe Playhouse. He was doing well at voiceovers, but this was not what he had spent three years training at the greatest drama school in the world for. The voiceovers were plentiful and he was solvent again. But all that meant was that he had time to think about what else to do.

There were qualifications he could take. He could retrain, just like the globalists said. Dustbin man this week, microbiologist the next. He could emigrate. He could become a day trader. He could join the Magic Circle. He could sell secret documents to the Chinese. The world was his to command. After all, most actors fell into new careers: getting a job in telesales, for example, and then spending twenty years as a call centre supervisor. Life was full of exciting possibilities. As for the entertainment industry, he knew his disillusion would only grow. He would keep an open mind but not make a decision yet. And so, he continued working, doing his voiceovers and keeping in touch with Melinda, while trying every now and then to establish contact with her mother.

One day, Niamh called him. This was an exciting development in itself.

'Hello, darling! How are you?'

'Getting back on track, thanks.'

'Yes, that was terrible what happened. People are bastards, aren't they?'

'Well, yes, some are.'

'You're very forgiving, dear one. If that had been me, I'd have hunted them down and flayed them alive.'

Troy didn't doubt it.

'You would too.'

'I bloody would. Now, angel heart, have you ever heard of Jerry Pilkington?'

'He's a politician, isn't he?'

Troy was embarrassed that he did not read the papers. He had other concerns and knowing about the many horrors of the world – if they hadn't been invented by the media in the first place – didn't make them get any better. But everyone had heard of Jerry Pilkington. He was an Independent MP who was famous for being accident prone and for saying the wrong thing at the wrong time. Everybody knew him: the papers and the crummy late-night comedians had a field day with him. He was probably a nice bloke, but he couldn't do right for doing wrong. The media roasted him on a spit when they couldn't think of any other news to manufacture. Poor Jerry Pilkington was the opposite of a national treasure.

'What about him?'

'Well, I'd never heard of him...'

Troy wasn't surprised about that.

'...but one of the big lookalike agencies contacted us last week. They wanted to know if I had anyone on my books who resembled him.'

Troy started to get an uneasy feeling. He tried to remember what Pilkington looked like.

'Well,' Niamh continued, 'they sent over some photos and guess what the stagecoach brought in?'

'Please, don't tell me I look like him.'

'Weeelllll, you'd have to get a crazy pair of specs and a silly ratting cap to cover up the fact that you're *not* bald, just as he wears one to cover up the fact that he *is*. But frankly my sweetness, he is *you* to the *life*.'

'Good grief! As if I don't have enough problems, I look like Jerry Pilkington. What do you want me to do? I'm not going to be his assassination double.'

'Watch a bit of telly. Try and see if you can get his voice off – I think he's from Plymouth or somewhere – talks like a pirate, you know. And when you've bought your accessories, come in and see me.'

'And then?'

'They've got about five jobs for you.'

'How much do they pay?'

Niamh told him and he was staggered. It was what he earned from voiceovers in a month.

'Much more work and money, if you can do the voice, darling.'

'Right. If you need me, I'll be at the opticians followed by the cap shop. After that, I'll be at the hospital having my larynx altered to sound like someone from Devon.'

'Good for you. I knew that method acting training would come in useful sometime. Lots of love and kisses. Thanks a million. See you soon, darling heart.'

Darling heart. He was darling heart while she had lots of work for him. If she hadn't, it would be *Miss Sullivan is in a meeting at the moment.*

Back to back all day I'm afraid but I'm sure she will be happy to call you as soon as she gets out…

And so, Troy began his new career doing exactly what he had wanted to break out of: namely, work which left him unsatisfied and anonymous, and which kept him as far away as possible from the big theatres and the good parts. But the money was absolutely ridiculous.

He did about eight engagements a week. He was so busy, he was turning down jobs. He was booked up weeks ahead. With a little practice and a few gags from a paid writer, he developed a comedy routine around the character. His fees went up as he was now not just a lookalike but an entertainment act. He did weddings, bar mitzvahs, company functions, corporate weekends and all sorts. Everything except funerals. Soon he was in a position to send Gloria her money. But he heard nothing back. He emailed Melinda and got a reply saying, 'Mommy says thanks for the money'.

He was soon back in the same position he had been in before Gudrun and Gosworth had fleeced him. But he was not happy.

CHAPTER THIRTY-FIVE

Melinda was crying. She was lying face down on her bed bawling. Gloria followed her into the room. She put her arm on her daughter's shoulder and said,

'Darling, I'm sorry. I wouldn't hurt you for the world.'

Melinda said nothing.

'Is it that you don't want me to get married or that you don't want me to marry Barry?'

'Both. I don't want you to marry anyone, but I don't like him.'

'Melinda, you know you'll always be the most important thing in the whole world for me. But I can't be lonely for the rest of my life. I do wish you could see that. I had to meet someone eventually.'

She paused.

'Why don't you like him?'

'He hates you.'

'He doesn't hate me; he loves me.'

'No, he doesn't.'

'Darling, I promise you that he won't come between us. I promise before God.'

'I want my daddy back.'

Gloria struggled to find a response to this. If her little daughter only knew how much this pained her. All she could say, as softly as possible, was,

'You know that can't happen. You must live with it. I've tried to resist it as a fact, but I couldn't. If we don't move on, we'll die or go mad. You have so much to look forward to in life. One day, you'll be happy. I know that.'

'No, I won't. I don't have anything to look forward to. Everything gets taken away. And I don't want to forget Daddy, ever.'

Gloria turned her daughter over and hugged her.

'Don't you love me?'

'Yes; that's why I don't want anyone to take you away. Something will, I know it will.'

'It won't. It won't ever. I promise.'

She felt awful making such promises: she knew she couldn't keep them. They were almost blasphemous. But Melinda calmed down.

'Are you going to see him tonight?'

'Yes, I'll be having dinner with him. Why don't you come?'

'No. I don't want to. I don't want you to go either.'

'Please try and understand, darling. You want me to be happy, don't you?'

Melinda nodded through her tears.

'Then please let me go. And we'll have the whole weekend together. That I can promise.'

She hugged and kissed her daughter again. Mrs K came in with some hot chocolate which Melinda liked.

'I won't be late back,' she said to Mrs K.

Gloria went back to her own room. She felt strangely tense and had been for a long time. Her life had so much pressure in it. The herbal tablets which Keeler had given her helped her to sleep, although she had to take three or four each night now to get the same effect. But she wasn't worried that they were dangerous. After all, they were only herbal medicine. They might even be placebo medication.

But she now found that she was feeling increasingly tense during the day. Barry had given her some other tablets which, he stressed again, were only harmless vegetable relaxants. But they were making her a bit groggy. She didn't feel that she was firing on all cylinders when at work. And the people around her were starting to notice. The director asked if she was feeling all right.

She said she was fine, just a little stressed. She had begun drinking a lot of coffee during the day to compensate. Eventually, she sent someone out to buy her some caffeine tablets. She was taking a lot of pills in one day. But it wasn't as though they were dangerous narcotics.

'You're overtired,' said Keeler as they had dinner that evening. 'Are you worried about the wedding? You're not having second thoughts, are you?'

'No, of course not. I love you and I'm looking forward to it, but it is a worry.'

She told him about Melinda. He understood perfectly.

'Of course, that's natural. She feels that I'm a threat. It's quite normal. She lost a father and now she feels that she might lose her mother. Who can blame her? But she'll get over it, I can assure you of that.'

'You're so understanding, Barry. Thank you for that.'

'We connect very well. I don't know why, but I feel strangely drawn to those who have known the incommunicable grief of having lost a spouse.'

'Yes, I'd forgotten; you're a widower too, aren't you?'

'Yes. She was a lot older than I was; and she was never well.'

'It's tragic. We take so much for granted: health, wealth, beauty, peace. It can all vanish in an instant.'

'You have wonderful insights,' he said. 'Are you OK now?'

'Yes, I'm just so tired.'

The caffeine that she pumped during the day was wearing off. She ordered some more coffee, knowing that she would be able to sleep at night, thanks to her herbal remedies.

CHAPTER THIRTY-SIX

It was the first time Melinda had been a bridesmaid. It should have been a memorable occasion, but it wasn't. She did not look happy. Nor did a lot of people who considered themselves friends of Gloria but were not invited. She hardly knew any of the guests, although she could not fault their generosity. The couple were up to their eyes in beautiful things, most of which they did not need. It is a moot point whether generosity is really a virtue for rich people. Indeed, in some cases, it can almost be a vice.

The wedding was held at a giant country club in Orange County, and although Keeler laid claim to religious beliefs, he had insisted on a civil ceremony to be performed at the club itself. There were a few children for Melinda to talk to. They all asked how much money her parents made. They seemed surprised when she replied that she didn't know.

Gloria looked beautiful, but did not wear a traditional wedding trousseau for her second marriage, just a designer gown flown in from Paris. There was no honeymoon, as Gloria was too busy. They arranged to travel to Europe later in the year. And so they settled down to what was supposed to be a normal married life.

Troy was hurt and depressed when he read about the wedding. He hadn't been invited. He still corresponded with Melinda, but even she hadn't told him. Had she been told not to? Or was he just an increasingly distant voice offstage? So distant that he no longer sounded important. Perhaps they assumed that he could not have afforded to come, which at the moment was not true.

However, he had much to occupy himself. He had been invited to a big extravaganza in aid of some new charity he had never heard of, dedicated to doing the same work that fifty other charities were already doing in the Third World. But he had decided that doing something for a charity was better than not doing it, so he happily agreed to do a free gig. His job, as usual, would be to do a 'guest appearance' of Jerry Pilkington. It was only a five-minute spot: there were a lot of acts coming and going.

When he arrived at the Lyceum Theatre in the West End, he went backstage and saw two people he knew vaguely. One was the comedian Den Dobson. Den was a small, aggressive man who laid claim to be a satirical commentator.

'Den! How are you?'

'Good, mate. Haven't seen you around for a while. Been working in the sticks?'

'Not seen me? I do the Jerry Pilkington act. I was on telly last night.'

'Was that you? Blimey! I never knew that.'

'Who did you think it was? Jerry Pilkington?'

'Wouldn't surprise me: he'll do anything for money.'

Troy was surprised to find himself feeling proprietorially defensive of the man he sent up for a living.

'Oh, I'm sure that's not true. He's a bit of a div, but he's not in it for the money. He means well.'

Dobson was not impressed.

'You think he'd come down and do a charity performance like this?'

Troy shrugged.

'Who knows? I wonder if anyone thought of asking him? But he'd probably get lost anyway.'

'You're naïve, mate. They're all bastards.'

Troy found himself shocked at this implacable harshness. At that moment, one of the organising assistants, a young man, walked past and said,

'Help yourself to the buffet. It's all got to go.'

'I thought that was for afterwards?' said Troy.

'I wouldn't wait that long with these gannets around,' said Dobson. 'Some of these clapped-out acts won't have eaten for a week.'

Troy laughed, although he did not share Dobson's brutal cynicism.

'I had a kebab before I came here. I wasn't expecting to be fed.'

'Get stuck in, mate,' said Dobson. 'Stick some in a bag and take it home with you. That's what I do.'

Another harassed-looking assistant came past. She was a middle-aged woman with a clipboard and was clearly trying to create some order out of chaos.

'Where the hell is the Jerry Pilkington act?' she bellowed.

'That's me,' said Troy.

She stopped and stared at him.

'You? You don't look anything like him.'

'Well...it is an act, and I am an actor.'

She threw up her eyes as if she had never met theatricals before.

'Well, could you get ready, please? You're on in ten.'

'I'm ready. I just put on the glasses and the cap.'

But she was gone - off to find a forgotten ventriloquist act.

Troy donned his accessories and took his place in the wings, next to Dobson who was on just before him. Behind himself, he could hear an altercation going on. He looked round. A famous TV personality was having an argument with the producer.

'I don't expect much at my time of life, but I do expect a dressing room I can stand up in.'

'I don't know what he's complaining about,' said Dobson. 'He could stand up in a shoe box.'

Strange to see Dobson making fun of a man for being as small as he was.

'...*And*,' the celebrity continued, 'I specifically told the girl on the phone that my fee should be in cash.'

'I'm sorry if there's been any misunderstanding,' the producer stammered, 'but this is a charity event.'

'I do lots of charity events. I'm highly sought after,' said the celebrity. 'This is the first time I've had a problem.'

'I'm sorry. I'm sure we can sort this out. Now we do have to get on.'

'If it isn't sorted now, there won't be an appearance.'

Troy was shocked. He turned to Dobson.

'Did you get a fee for turning up tonight?'

'No way,' replied the comic. He stared at the celebrity and said, 'Greedy bastard.'

Then he turned back to Troy and said, 'No, no fee. Just expenses. I come from a long way off. I live in Buckinghamshire.'

'Nice place. I didn't think it was that far. You get expenses?'

'Yeah, sure. Didn't you?'

'No.'

'Did you ask?'

'No, of course not.'

'You must be an idiot.'

'And another thing,' the celebrity was saying, 'Do you call that a buffet? I've seen better spreads down the seaman's mission.'

Dobson was called on stage and began his act. He only had five minutes which he mostly filled with expletives. He made two vicious jokes about a member of the Royal Family who had been involved in a car crash. Troy walked to the exit, pausing only to throw his cap and glasses into the waste bin. He was done with show business.

CHAPTER THIRTY-SEVEN

'Where the hell is Melinda?' asked Keeler gruffly, as they were breakfasting on the patio one morning.

'She's in her room,' said Gloria, startled by his uncharacteristic anger.

'She's always in her room. Why doesn't she come down occasionally?'

'She's a young girl, darling,' she replied pacifically. 'She's probably on the phone to all her friends.'

'Does she have any friends? It's not natural. There's plenty to do in this house. Do you know how much it costs to run that damn pool? I should drain the damn thing. Nobody ever uses it.'

'Barry, what's wrong with you? I've never seen you like this. Is there something the matter?'

'That girl is something the matter.'

He threw aside the paper he was reading.

''I'm sorry,' he said, in a calmer tone. 'It gives me the creeps the way she avoids me. I feel like an intruder in my own house.'

'But darling, you said yourself she'd get used to it. You said it was just a phase.'

'Well, I didn't expect it to last this long.'

'A few weeks, Barry. Give her some time. She'll come round.'

'She'd better. It's just not right. I'll see you later.'

He rose from the table and kissed her as if they had been married for twenty years. He left to go to whatever vague and ill-defined activity he called work, leaving Gloria quite upset.

She went upstairs and peeped round Melinda's bedroom door.

'Can I come in?'

'Of course you can, mom. You know you can always come in.'

Melinda was lying on a large bed with an opalescent duvet. Her mother sat next to her and put her arm around her.

'Are you all right?'

'I'm OK.'

'You don't come out much. You have the run of this huge, lovely house and you don't go anywhere.'

'I liked our house better.'

'We have to get used to changes in our lives, darling. Barry's gone to work now so you can come downstairs.'

'What does he do, mom?'

Gloria found it difficult to put it into the kind of words a young girl would understand, so she said,

'He's in business.'

But she wondered if she would have been able to explain it to an adult. Eventually, Melinda came down and went for a swim. But the situation did not get better.

'And another thing,' yelled Keeler a few nights later at dinner, 'I don't like that Polish woman. She gives me the creeps, moping about the place like a damned Golem.'

Gloria was shocked again. She had never seen him like this before and he seemed to be getting worse. Everything seemed to upset him. And he had never used language like that before their marriage. But when she mentioned it later that night to Mrs K, the Polish woman simply said,

'He is not changing. This is the real him. I was waiting to see it.'

'Oh, no, Mrs K. That can't be true. I know him.'

'Not yet, Mrs Newton. But you will.'

'I'm Mrs Keeler now.'

But Mrs K kept right on calling her Mrs Newton.

'What kind of work are you looking for, Troy?'

'That's a very good question,' he replied. 'I really am open to suggestions.'

He was being interviewed at the offices of Top Notch Resource Recruitment UK, a large national employment agency. There was a pause. Sandra, the interviewer, wasn't really in the mood for people who were after careers advice. The company made its money matching up CVs to known vacancies. Sometimes, the match-ups were a bit surreal, but it was a strange business. Often the wrong candidates hit it off with the wrong employer and got the job for which they weren't really suited. You didn't get anywhere in such a competitive business without taking chances.

'I *am* a graduate. I did three years at RADA.'

'Well, that's great. What sort of a degree would that be?'

Troy couldn't believe it: she had never heard of RADA.

'Erm...drama and English. You know, acting and the performing arts. That sort of thing.'

'I see,' she said. Troy wasn't encouraged by the way she said *I see*. She rather gave the impression of seeing something she didn't have any use for.

'Great,' she added. Then she paused to have a think.

'You might have to retrain. A lot of people do these days.'

'Yes, I'll do that. What should I retrain as?'

Sandra was having a little difficulty making this man see that she wasn't there to provide free life coaching.

'I really don't know. Perhaps you should have a think about it and then you can come back and see us. In the meantime, I'll keep your CV on file and if anything comes up for which you might be suited, we can give you a call.'

Sandra beamed with finality and then stood up to signal that the interview was over. Troy stood up too. But he didn't leave.

'What do people retrain as?'

'Well, lots of things: IT, accountancy… If you're a graduate, you could retrain as an accountant. But it wouldn't be anything like as much fun as theatrical work and show business.'

'Don't you believe it.'

As Troy was still lingering, she tried another tactic.

'Any questions before you go?'

'Yes, what time do you get off work?'

She paused, before saying, '5.30'.

'OK, I'll see you in that pub across the road.'

She paused again and then said, 'All right.'

CHAPTER THIRTY-EIGHT

Only a few months after Gloria married Barry Keeler, an unexpected incident occurred. Police in Las Vegas, Nevada, stopped a man who seemed to be driving even more erratically than Americans usually drive. He gave his name as Mr Umran Khan and his occupation as astrological investigator. A quick check on their records revealed that his name was actually Ulysses Cahn and that he was originally from Yonkers, New York State. He had a previous conviction for wire fraud. His car was searched and was found to contain a quantity of barbiturates and amphetamines. Khan or Cahn was in big trouble, so he decided to make a deal with the authorities as he had, he said, many an interesting tale to tell.

On the basis of one of his stories, the police in Clark County, Nevada obtained an order for the exhumation of Mrs Desdemona Keeler, the former wife of Mr Barry Keeler, now residing in Los Angeles. An autopsy was performed and the coroner concluded that Mrs Keeler had not died from a heart attack at all, but from severe narcotic poisoning, possibly caused by an overdose of barbiturates. It was suspected that the doctor who had signed the death certificate had been suborned. The late Mrs Keeler had been a wealthy widow when she had married Keeler and he had inherited her money and house. The police interviewed people who had known her, who said that she had seemed groggy and out of sorts towards the end.

The police then came to Keeler's house and he was arrested. Gloria was horrified. Mrs K wasn't in the least surprised. They asked if the suspect had given her any medication at all. She gave them all the herbal remedies which Keeler had provided and, after forensic analysis, they were revealed to be powerful barbiturates and tranquilisers. She was advised to check into a clinic to have her dependency reduced.

A few weeks after the scandal broke, her show *StarGirl* was cancelled. It had run for many episodes and she had made more than enough money from it; but ratings were starting to decline and it was a family show which did not want any connection with drugs and scandal. Clearly her career had reached its zenith. Other offers came in for Gloria, but not so often and they were all less well paid.

Troy kept in touch with Melinda. He told her he was retraining as an accountant, so when he was very rich and she had her qualifications, he would give her a job. But her replies became less and less frequent and eventually, he stopped hearing from her completely. She and her mother eventually re-located back to the UK, but Troy could never find out where.

CHAPTER THIRTY-NINE

It was 2015. Gloria sat in the offices of Temple and Fortune publishing house, kneading her handbag like a schoolgirl awaiting the results of a pregnancy test. This was one of many new experiences for her. In her twenties, Gloria had not had to hang around in waiting rooms to see people. People came to see her; and although she had never been so rude as to keep them waiting, she could have. Now it seemed that she was being repaid for a haughtiness she had never displayed. Occasionally, the receptionist looked up and smiled with painful awkwardness.

'I'm sure Mr Green won't be too much longer.'

'That's quite all right,' she replied. 'I'm sure he's very busy.'

The receptionist nodded, but this time without smiling. Someone so understanding couldn't possibly be anyone of consequence. Gloria had been sitting there for twenty minutes now. She felt like getting up and leaving, but she knew she couldn't. She wasn't exactly desperate for money, but she needed it nonetheless. She had a daughter to think of as well as her own future. She had to strike a deal while people still remembered her.

Eventually, she was shown into a plush office. Jeff Green was a man barely any older than herself but running prematurely to middle-age spread. He clearly lived well from his job, although you wouldn't have known it from his scruffy apparel, which consisted of sweatshirt and ripped jeans. He was charming but gave the impression of being pushed for time.

'Yes, Gloria – can I call you Gloria? – thank you. I got your email. I'm really sorry that you weren't satisfied with the offer, but I'm afraid this is the reality of the publishing industry at the moment. It's a very tight market.'

Gloria smiled and said,

'Yes, I quite understand. It's just that – well, I know you shouldn't believe anything you read in the papers – but I rather got the impression that show business memoirs sold for very large amounts.'

'In some cases, yes, they do. It depends who the star is. Perhaps you read about Sheena Grace?'

'Yes; she got half a million for hers.'

He nodded quickly. He was quick to agree with her whenever he could. 'You're dead right about the papers; they exaggerate like hell. It probably wasn't anything like that. But whatever it was, you see she's quite hot at the moment. That's the decider. Quick in, quick out. Make a killing while they're hot, because – well, I don't need to tell you how fast things change in show business.'

'You certainly don't. Are you saying I should have written my memoirs when I was twenty-three?'

'It's an interesting idea. Negotiate a price for a work in progress and get the money up front. A bit like the futures market.'

'I didn't think of that at the time.'

'Well, let's not spend the day dreaming of things that might have been. I'm afraid this is all we can offer at the moment.'

He leaned forward, putting his elbows on the desk, in what he hoped suggested a compromising posture.

'If you don't mind me mentioning it, you must have made a lot of money in your early years.'

'Yes, I'm not claiming utter penury, but my daughter and I still have our lives ahead of us. She's twelve and I'm nowhere near forty yet. The people who knew me can't all have died.'

'Well, that's exactly my point: you haven't lived half your life yet, so your memoirs are necessarily… you know… incomplete… a work in progress. We're only buying half a life story.'

He smiled as if she would be amused by this flippancy. Then he continued,

'I don't have to tell you how fickle the public is. Do you ever watch soap operas?'

'Yes, sometimes.'

'The people who watch them can't remember the names of their stars even while they're famous. They say, 'Look, there's whatshername' when they see them in the street. And they hardly know the difference between Lady Macbeth and Lady Gaga.'

Green pointedly looked at his watch and Gloria realised that they were just going round in circles. Moreover, she felt that she was close to begging, which is never a good tactic in business. She hadn't given enough thought to pressing an argument about how good her memoirs would be for the company. She knew nothing of business or the real world she had never really lived in.

'Don't be downcast, Gloria. After all, we're only talking about an advance here. If the book sells, you'll be quids in. But we just don't offer huge advances in a case like this.'

'Will you help me promote it?'

'You bet! We certainly will. We'll organise a few radio interviews and we'll get you out on promotional tours and book signings. We're old hands at show business books. That's our forte.'

'That's very helpful. Thank you.'

'No problem at all. Glad to help,' he said, getting up from his chair and again looking at his watch.

'We'll be in touch,' he said as he opened the office door for her. He didn't see her to the exit.

Troy had not seen Gloria for ages when he ran into her at the end of the year. He was browsing in a Waterstones bookshop in Earl's Court, when he was surprised to see her sitting at a desk signing copies of her autobiography entitled *StarGirl*. Or rather, she was waiting to sign copies for anyone who came up and asked. He went up to her. She looked up and smiled at him. Troy wasn't sure if it was his imagination but her once refulgent smile seemed slightly dimmed now. Yet she couldn't have been more than thirty-three.

'Hello,' he said. 'Still signing autographs? That's a good sign.'

Gloria smiled again and Troy realised in amazement that she had not recognised him. Had he changed that much? He still had all his hair, and it was a long way from going grey. That surprise was as of nothing, however, when she reached out and took the book he was holding, opened it at the front page and signed it for him.

'Whose name shall I put?' she asked sweetly.

He was devastated.

'Gloria, it's me, Troy.'

'Yes, of course. Troy.'

'Troy. As in the ten-year siege. Troy Colson.'

She wrote in the book, *To Troy with love and best wishes, Gloria Greatorex.*

'Thank you, Troy. I do hope you enjoy it.'

She closed the book and gave it back to him. He looked at the cover. *You and Your Allotment.* He hadn't even bought it yet.

'Thanks, Gloria. I'm sure I will.'

He started to say something to her, but she was already signing someone else's book.

He never saw her again.

CHAPTER FORTY

The next day, Troy went to another bookshop nearby and bought a copy of *StarGirl*. The assistant wasn't sure if they had one and she had to check on the computer. Troy was pleased that they did. He bought two copies and took them home.

He had a tough schedule at work for a few days, so he decided to read it at the weekend. On the way home on Friday, Sandra, the recruitment consultant and now his wife, called him while he was on the train. She was a voracious reader and had nearly finished the book.

'I thought you knew this woman.'

'Knew her? We all had a very special bond. Why?'

'Well, you're not mentioned anywhere.'

'What? Well...I mean, we weren't childhood friends so she may not have got to the part when we met. It wasn't until 2001.'

'I'm at 2012 and she's got thirty pages to fit you in.'

On Saturday, Troy deferred all his errands and jobs in order to read the whole book from cover to cover. Not only was he not mentioned, but the rest of the book was a complete fantasy. Stories which could never have happened and anecdotes which seemed familiar from other people's lives abounded. But there was nothing about Troy, very little about Shirley – Gloria had apparently begged her not to go to the stunt audition – and Leonard was an unrecognisable paragon of humility and selflessness.

The UFO incident was mentioned. It was covered in a great deal of detail. Great significance was drawn out of it, both as an astrological portent and as a scientific phenomenon. Troy hadn't been present at the time and so could not have pointed out that it was a military jet. Leonard had been sceptical, but she had convinced him that it was real. *Well, lucky Leonard*, he thought. *At least he's had some kind of tribute.* Sandra tried to console him. Her wide reading allowed her to shed some light on the affair.

'This is way more common than you think. For a start, these books are written by ghostwriters...'

'...This wasn't – I recognised her style...'

'...but even when they aren't, they are often written and edited for readability and excitement.'

'Well, yes, thanks. I suppose if excitement is a concern, then naturally you would want my existence completely excised.'

She sat next to him and stroked his head.

'Oh, darling, don't be upset.'

She reminded him of the *Naked Civil Servant* by Quentin Crisp. When it was published, his best friend in the world, Joan Rhodes, the beautiful strongwoman, came to the launch and lifted him up on her shoulders for a publicity stunt. Yet there is no mention of her anywhere in that book or anywhere else in his writings.

'They were best friends for about sixty years until he died and he never mentioned her.'

'Why not?'

Sandra shrugged.

'It just wasn't part of the story he wanted to tell.'

'OK, so it happens. That doesn't make it right.'

'No.'

'Most of this book is rubbish.'

'Try not to be too upset. Posterity is a synonym for mythology, dear.'

CHAPTER FORTY-ONE

In January 2016, Troy was at work, browsing the internet, which he shouldn't have been doing. The BBC site said, *David Bowie Dead.*
'No, he isn't,' said Troy to himself. 'Everyone knows he's still alive.'
But he was dead. To be followed shortly by Alan Rickman. One by one, as the curious year progressed, celebrities and stars were dying at an extraordinary rate. So many died that people were using the word 'now' when telling people.
'*Bloody hell!* They would say, *Now it's Ronnie Corbett!*
Then it was Prince, Victoria Wood and so on.
He would be talking about it to Sandra when another would come through: Mohammad Ali, Gene Wilder, Zsa Zsa Gabor, Sir George Martin. The celebrities of the world were going down like front-line soldiers. Everywhere Troy looked that year, he was surrounded by reminders of the mortality of the supposed immortals; especially as he found himself visiting a hospital on a regular basis.

It wasn't that Troy didn't like hospitals – at least no more than anyone else – but he had had enough of death and suffering for one lifetime. He didn't want to go to see his Aunt Marnie. He was not close to her; indeed, he hardly knew her. But his mother herself was too ill to go and see her sister-in-law, so he had been standing in. Aunt Marnie had a strange purpose for wanting him to come and see her.
As usual, she was in a different ward from the last visit. He found her in an isolated room at the end of a corridor. That fact itself did not bode well. Not that he was in any doubt about her impending fate. She had

lost so much weight that she almost resembled a corpse. She lay face upwards with her emaciated arms lying outside the bed. He leaned over and said quietly, 'Aunt Marnie?' She was amazingly lucid for someone *in extremis*. She could still hear and understand him.

'Troy?'

'Yes, it's me.'

'Who now?'

'Gene Wilder. The American actor and alleged comedian. His death came through while I was discussing the issue with Sandra.'

He said that too quickly and quietly for her to understand but she caught the name.

'Do you understand what is happening, Troy?'

'I'm not sure what you mean, Aunt Marnie.'

'No, you wouldn't. God is culling the false gods of the world. So many in one year. It is a sign…Something is coming…Mark my words, something is coming.'

'What is it that is coming, Aunt Marnie?'

She breathed harshly for a few moments. Then she said,

'He does this for a purpose.'

'What purpose is that, Aunt Marnie?'

She seemed to be struggling for enough breath to tell him. Perhaps the answer was long and complicated. But he would never know what it was. At that moment, she stopped breathing and was gone.

On September 11th of that year, Troy left his bewildered wife to go out and have a meal on his own. He drank a toast to his absent friends but didn't eat much.

He found it difficult to remember what this lustrum was originally meant to commemorate, now that it had become an observance of lost love and unspeakable anguish. He felt sure that it must have been intended to celebrate the realisation of their vibrant and unstoppable young dreams. And now, all that expectant joy was gone, like ice thawed in a false spring. And so he drank a new toast to the *Ice Idols*. To Shirley, intoxicated with optimism to the point where it was almost a personality disorder. To Leonard, who needed so much to be noticed, if not for good then for bad. And to Gloria, who was seized and abducted by a tide of fame she was unable to understand and powerless to control, then poisoned by the parasites who infested that toxic world. And all of them dwarfed by the talents they possessed; talents which were fated to have an irresistible effect on their lives, over and above the fickle and cruel operations of life itself. He hoped and prayed that Melinda would be ordinary; that she would live in a world where the snares and temptations would be proportionate to what the human spirit can bear. It wasn't until the waiter asked him if he was all right that he noticed that he had been crying.

The last celebrity to die on December 28th of that year was Debbie Reynolds, just a day after her famous daughter, Carrie Fisher, had died, and three days after singer George Michael.

It was in the spring of 2018 that Troy and Sandra were walking around the British Museum when he saw Melinda. She would be about fifteen now. She looked well and was blossoming into an attractive young woman. She recognised Troy – after he had reminded her who he was – and seemed glad to see him.

He introduced her to Sandra and told her whose daughter she was.

'Good heavens!' Sandra said. 'I thought you'd only done voiceovers. You never told me you knew big celebrities.'

'What? You know very well I...Oh, yes. I've known many famous names in my life. But I wasn't that big myself. I'm glad I'm out of it. I bet you are too, aren't you, Melinda?'

Melinda smiled and shrugged and said, 'I guess so.'

'How's your mum?'

'She's fine. She doesn't go out much.'

'I'd like to hear from her. I really would. Just a line.'

He gave Melinda his new address and telephone number. She took them and said,

'Sure, I'll ask her.'

But she said no more, and Troy felt that he shouldn't force the issue.

'And what are you planning to do with your life?' asked Sandra. 'Will you go into acting too?'

'No!' Troy almost shouted. 'No way. Don't give her ideas.'

He was relieved when Melinda said,

'I'm interested in anthropology.'

'I did psychology,' said Sandra.

'Yes; it helps with our marriage,' said Troy. Sandra shushed him and asked,

'Is that why you're here?'

'I guess so. I love looking at these strange carvings.'

She indicated a hideous ornate wooden fetish from some ancient, collapsed civilisation.

'People used to worship them. I wonder why?'

'I know,' said Troy. 'It's because the real God is too big for them.'

Melinda politely said it was nice seeing them, but not as if it had been the highlight of the season. She apologised and said that she had to go.

Troy was about to remind her to get Gloria to call him, but he realised there was no point. Gloria was gone forever. She had touched the sun, but her wings had melted. Better to leave her where she was. Better to remember her as a luminous heavenly body than as a collapsed star. He had wanted to say more to Melinda, to take an interest in her life, but she was gone too, taking with her the last of whatever the four of them had had together.

CHAPTER FORTY-TWO

One day, while Troy was making his way reluctantly to the hospital, he saw a derelict sitting on the corner of the Tottenham Court Road. The man looked as if he had once been healthy and handsome, but was now reduced to begging. He was holding a coffee cup with a little bit of money in it. Troy felt in his pocket for some of his own change and leaned over to put it in the cup. It was only when he bent down that he recognised the unshaven tramp as Ted Gosworth. They stared at each other for a few moments, then Gosworth lowered his eyes to look at the pavement. Neither of them said anything for a while until Troy asked,
'How long did the money last? My money, I mean.'
Gosworth didn't speak for a minute, then he said,
'I never saw it. We arranged to meet somewhere but she never turned up. She had all the cash. I never saw her again after I left your flat.'
Troy looked at the change in his hand for a few seconds, then dropped it into the cup and walked on.

As a general rule, Troy preferred the dentist to the hospital, even when it was just a routine check-up. The doctor, a young woman called Dr Akhtar, who looked to his aging eye like a teenager, was at pains to reassure him. She failed. She slung her stethoscope over her green shoulders. Doctors and nurses were now a lot different from the old days. In the old movies, they used to look very glamorous. Now they looked like they worked in the engine room of a spaceship.
'The worst possible diagnosis is uncertainty,' she said.
'Yes. I am quite of your opinion.'

'The problem with heart murmurs is that they can be completely harmless or they could be indicative of something far more serious. That makes it a quite different ailment from er...'

She paused to think of an appropriate comparison.

'Being shot in the back?'

'...that makes it a quite different ailment from most others where we have a much more certain diagnosis.'

'Right.'

'Well, the murmur on the heart is not in doubt. What we have to ascertain is whether it is accompanied by any other symptoms.'

'OK, I'm game.'

'Any dizziness?'

'No, I don't think so.'

'Cough?'

'Occasionally, but I'm not a fanatic.'

'But you've never smoked?'

'No.'

'Chest pains?'

'Sometimes, but not really bad.'

The catechism continued for a few minutes. Some of the symptoms he had, some he hadn't. None of them was serious but they were there all the same.

'We'll have to do some further tests.'

'Of course. What does it all mean?'

'It means it might be nothing, but it could be something.'

'That's good: I feel better already.'

'Mostly it is nothing to worry about but...'

'Yes, I know - but I'll start worrying just in case. That way I'll be ahead of the game if it does turn out to be serious.'

She inspected his details.

'Oh, it's your birthday tomorrow.'

'It is.'

She typed something quietly.

'I've put you in for a chest X-ray.'

'Very good of you. Some people only send a card.'

As he walked home, he was aware of a strong sense of unease about the world, although he realised that it may have had personal origins. So far, the plagues and wars of the end had not materialised. At least, there were none on the horizon yet. There were plenty *over* the horizon, as there always were, but he selfishly thought that that was where they belonged, while complacently believing that that was where they would stay.

It was 2019 and it would be his birthday tomorrow. He was, he told himself, only thirty-nine. But he had realised that you should never prefix an age with 'only'. It didn't make any sense. Some people died when they were twenty. Some people graduated when they were ninety. A few moments difference here and there, so that it was fatuous to talk about living longer or to an old age. Sometimes that little flicker of life was an ephemeral spark and sometimes it was the fading glow of a small ember. Sometimes, in rare cases, it was the incandescent flash of a comet across the night sky. But the difference was measured in seconds and existed only in the memory thereafter. And what use was the memory, if it remembered only delusions?

Somewhere, perhaps in fifty years' time, Gloria would be telling people that she had once seen a UFO. And in her mind, she had. There might be people who were prepared to believe that she had seen an extra-terrestrial spacecraft, but would refuse to believe that she had once been world famous. And, with shaky, arthritic hands, she would pull out tatty newspaper clippings to prove it, and to remind herself as much as anyone else.

Troy would never see her again. And that meant that, like Leonard, but unlike Shirley, he would only bear the grief and pain of losing her once.

Printed and bound by CPI Group (UK) Ltd, Croydon, CR0 4YY
06/04/2024
03764952-0001